Her awareness that love was the most dangerous thing in the world felt more threatening than the raging storm.

That just felt *wrong*. To be thinking of Trevor and love in the same sentence. He was Caitlyn's.

But what did that mean *now*?

Stop it, Jacey told herself. If anything, Caitlyn's death and his suffering, and her own, just proved her point. Love *was* the most dangerous threat of all.

Still, what did it mean to her relationship with Trevor now that Caitlyn was gone? Did it have to mean anything? Did everything have to mean something? Did her whole life have to be a study in the seriousness of unintended consequences? Did she have to ferret out catastrophe because it had visited her in the past?

Of course not. She could consciously decide not to be timid, couldn't she? Jacey was aware she needed to accept this gift in the spirit it had been given.

Was it not possible to just relax and enjoy the unexpected adventure? Even being caught in a storm with an extremely capable guy could be interpreted as an adventure instead of a harbinger of doom, couldn't it? What was it *other* people said?

Enjoy the moment.

Dear Reader,

I grew up in Calgary, Alberta, in the shadow of the Canadian Rocky Mountains. My step-grandfather, Edward Day, was born and raised in Banff. I recall an old photo of him ski jumping at Mount Norquay.

My sisters, Anna and Avon, and I were introduced to skiing at a young age at Calgary's ski hill, Paskapoo. It would go on to become Canada Olympic Park when Calgary hosted the 1988 Winter Olympics.

We considered Banff and Kananaskis Country our backyard, and we spent our teens and early adult years skiing the greats: Fortress Mountain; Mount Norquay; Lake Louise; and of course, Sunshine Village, the resort the fictional Moonbeam of this story is loosely based on.

My older sister, Avon, like the heroine of this story, was "small but mighty." Her innate strength was particularly evident on the ski hill. I was the less athletic tagalong, trailing her down the slopes, longing to go in for hot chocolate, while she scorned taking a break in favor of "one more run."

Whether you have skied all your life or not at all, I hope you'll experience some of the power, majesty and magic of the mountains in the backdrop of this story.

With warmest wishes, as always,

Cara Colter

Snowed In with the Billionaire

Cara Colter

Recycling programs for this product may not exist in your area.

ISBN-13: 978-1-335-73692-5

Snowed In with the Billionaire

Copyright © 2022 by Cara Colter

Harlequin Enterprises ULC
22 Adelaide St. West, 41st Floor
Toronto, Ontario M5H 4E3, Canada
www.Harlequin.com

Printed in U.S.A.

Cara Colter shares her home in beautiful British Columbia, Canada, with her husband of more than thirty years, an ancient, crabby cat and several horses. She has three grown children and two grandsons.

In memory of Avon

1956–2019

Praise for
Cara Colter

"Ms. Colter's writing style is one you will want to continue to read. Her descriptions place you there.... This story does have [an] HEA but leaves you wanting more."

—*Harlequin Junkie* on *His Convenient Royal Bride*

PROLOGUE

Jacey Tremblay shut the door of her apartment and looked down, with a frown, at the rectangular eight-by-ten cardboard envelope in her hand.

Registered.

In her experience, nothing good ever came by registered mail. Her divorce decree, of several months ago, being a case in point.

She turned the letter over in her hands. It was from a law firm she had never heard of, which made her dread worsen.

Obviously, she was being sued. By someone. For something.

She took a deep breath. Who sued a music tutor?

Johnny Jordan's parents, of course. They had entrusted her with their protégé. Given her first-hand experience, she should have known that was not going to work out!

Fourteen-year-old Johnny, musically brilliant, had not gained admission to the Canadian Academy for Betterment of the Arts. That was despite near perfection on that devilishly difficult Chopin piece they had rehearsed for his audition.

Really? Jacey should have warned his parents she was something of an expert on failed protégés!

No, it wasn't that, she told herself, but doubtfully. While turning the envelope over in her hands, she scanned her mind for other possibilities.

What about that little fender bender on Bloor? Jacey had exchanged insurance information with a delightful geriatric, who had accepted all the blame and admitted she had pulled right out of her parking spot without shoulder checking or signaling. There had never been another word, and that had been at least three months ago.

But that didn't mean said granny hadn't died, or suffered an after-injury that she or her family were now suing for.

With her heart racing at the endless possibilities for catastrophe to visit her life, Jacey took the envelope and sat down on her love seat, which acted as the sofa in her tiny apartment. It was white with a backdrop print of large purple pansies. She had purchased the piece of furniture after the divorce, in a futile attempt to find the bright side in the failure of her marriage.

See? I don't have to consult anyone about what furniture I buy. Her ex, Bruce, who in retrospect she could see had been stingy with his approval, would have hated every single thing about the love seat: form, function and especially the flamboyant color.

She turned her attention, resolutely, back to the envelope.

"Not this week," Jacey told it firmly. "It's a bad time."

So bad, she had taken the week off and canceled on all of her students. Given her failure with Johnny, her most promising student ever, she was not sure she should go back to teaching music. The local supermarket around the corner always had a help-wanted sign up...

But a new career was for next week. This week she had laid into an extra-large bucket of Neapolitan ice cream and bought new comfy pajamas. The pajamas, covered in adorable cartoon kittens, were, like the sofa, a statement about not needing to care what anyone thought.

Jacey had also made a list of movies she planned to watch. It was a shorter list than what she had hoped for, as she had crossed anything romantic, and anything sad, off her list.

"Open it," she commanded herself, turning her attention, again, to the envelope.

For some reason they made these kinds of official-looking packets extremely hard to get into. But finally, Jacey wrestled a single slip of paper and a bulkier brown envelope from the now mangled packaging.

Surprise!

She felt the blood drain from her face as she continued reading the familiar handwriting.

...and I know nobody hates a surprise more than you.

CHAPTER ONE

"GO AWAY," Trevor Cooper called, annoyed, from his prone position on the couch. "Unless you have pizza. Then you can just drop it on the doorstep."

Not that he'd ordered pizza, though come to think of it, that wasn't a bad idea. He tilted his head, looking away from the three side-by-side wall-mounted TV sets, where he was, thanks to the miracle of modern electronics, keeping a close eye on several sporting events simultaneously.

And keeping his mind off what day this was.

Maybe ordering pizza was not such a great idea. His huge open-concept living room, dining area and kitchen was already littered with greasy empty boxes, begging the question: *Could man live on pizza alone?*

Apparently, he could.

Even when he didn't want to. Live, that was. Because two years ago today, his reason for living had gone.

The knock came again, persistent. Trevor thought, crankily, he shouldn't be paying exor-

bitant gated community fees to be fielding un-
announced solicitors at the door, because, Lord
knew, he was not expecting company.

When the knock came the third time, he unfolded himself from the couch, glanced down at
his naked chest and low-hanging pajama bottoms,
and stalked across the room. It was not appropriate to answer your door half-naked, especially in
an upscale estate neighborhood like this one, and
as he flung open the door he had the thought, *but
what if it's that little girl from down the street,
selling Girl Scout cookies?* A neighbor knocking
would explain the breeching of the security sys-
tem that made getting into Calgary's tony Mountain View Villas akin to getting into Fort Knox.

But as it turned out, it wasn't a wide-eyed Girl
Scout.

It was imminently worse.

"Jacey," he said. Inside he cursed. If there was
one person he did not want seeing him like this—
disheveled, unshaven, only partially dressed in
the middle of the day—it was her.

Or maybe his concern wasn't so much for his
appearance, but for that of the house. The outside
grounds, of course, were impeccably kept by the
community association. The gatehouse, just visible in the distance, was winter-themed, like a
dollhouse. In the central man-made lake, which
his house fronted, the fountain had been replaced

for winter with an extravagant ice sculpture of a mother grizzly bear trailed by two cubs.

No, it wasn't his state of undress, or the state of the house. It was the *day*.

"Trevor," she said.

He let the uncomfortable silence bleed between them.

"The gatehouse didn't call," he said, aware his tone was faintly accusing.

"Interesting," she said, mildly. "I thought maybe your phone was broken, permanently set to off, or at the bottom of that lake."

"You can't order pizza without a phone."

"Does it come by cab? That's probably why we were waved through the gate."

She sidestepped slightly, to squint into the dimness behind him. He thought he detected disapproval in her look. He folded his arms over his naked chest and planted his feet, a *go-away* stance if ever there was one.

She ignored the message. Completely.

"May I come in?"

"No!" There. If she couldn't get the subtle messages of his body posture, he'd have to be forthright.

He didn't want her to see the house. How could she not think his neglect was a desecration of Caitlyn's dream house?

Trevor hated it when this happened—unexpected flashes of memory. And he especially hated it today. But there it was, the image of him and Caitlyn entering this house for the first time. Her wide eyes, her excited laughter, her tears of joy.

This is what he could expect from a visit with Jacey. The very thing he had been running from for two years.

Memories.

People said the first year was the worst, but Trevor was not sure he believed that. People said time healed all wounds, and he didn't believe that, either.

"You should have called," he said, though, in fact, despite the mess the house was in, he could not deny the sense of connection he felt with Jacey Tremblay that he probably would never feel with another human being. They had been through a war together.

"I tried," she said, and lifted her chin at him. "Apparently, your phone is used exclusively for pizza delivery."

It was true. His phone had been set to go straight to voice mail for a couple of days. He hadn't checked them. Still, he wasn't apologizing.

"Maybe you should have taken that as a hint."

Something in the deliberate braveness of her expression faltered, and Trevor felt the smallest niggling of something.

Shame. Jacey lived over three thousand miles away from Calgary in Toronto. She'd obviously made a huge effort—misguided as it was—to be with him for this awful second anniversary.

She had been the one, of all their friends, and all their family, who had never shirked. Who had stayed the course. She'd given up her music clients and abandoned her husband to be there in those final weeks for her best friend—his wife—when she was dying of cancer. Jacey had made it possible for Caitlyn to be here, in the home she had loved, right until the end.

Which had not been pretty, but this woman had not flinched.

Trevor took Jacey in. Even under a trench coat that didn't look warm enough for this cold day and that hid most of her—Caitlyn had always said of her friend she was small and had no idea how mighty she was—she looked even more slender than he remembered.

She had cut her blond hair short, and it was sticking up in spikes all over her head, whether from travel or by design he had no idea. Her ears, exposed by the new haircut, were tiny, like a doll's, and pink from not wearing a hat in the January chill. The haircut also made her eyes look huge and showed her features to be gamine.

She had applied the lightest dusting of makeup. It didn't cover that spattering of freckles across her pert nose, or the shadows under—or in—those green eyes.

Why had Jacey come here?

She was obviously travel rumpled and tired. And yet, even underneath those things, he recognized something of himself in the expression in those deep green eyes.

Unrelenting sorrow.

So much for time healing all wounds.

His sense of shame at the abruptness of his greeting deepened. He had a sudden awareness of how angry Caitlyn would be with him for this lukewarm—make that as ice-cold as this January day—greeting to her dearest and most loyal friend.

Still, *shame* was a feeling, and as such it felt dangerous.

And anger, more powerful, now battled with it.

If Caitlyn wanted him to be a better man, she should have stuck around to finish the job she had started.

The shame swept forward again. How could he act as if she'd had a choice? She didn't want cancer. She would have done anything to stay in this life they had built together, to have those babies she had been so desperate for.

So it wasn't Caitlyn he was angry at.

And not Jacey, either.

It was the whole world. It was his powerlessness, his fury at himself and his inability to change anything when it had truly mattered.

Really? This world—this dark space he was

in, that he tried to shut out with games and multiple television sets—was no world to invite Jacey into, no matter how rude that seemed; no matter how good her intentions in coming.

He ran a hand through his hair. "Look, it's not a good day."

"You think I don't know it's not a good day?" she asked, incredulous and miffed.

And yet, even knowing that, there she stood. She didn't wait for him to finish his explanation, or for an invitation. She put a hand on his naked chest. It felt as if it burned him. Shouldn't her hand be cold, since she was standing outside on a frosty morning without gloves on?

Before he could come up with a defensive maneuver, Jacey shoved him. Given her size, her strength was shocking, and for the first time he noticed a rather frightening detail. One of those wheeled suitcases followed her like an obedient puppy as she marched right by him and into the deeply shadowed house.

She paused and took it all in. The darkness of pulled shades, the pizza boxes, the rumpled clothes on the floor, the layers of dust, the film of sadness everywhere.

He reluctantly closed the door against the blast of cold air that came in with her and then turned and stared, not at her, but at her suitcase. It wasn't one of those tiny ones that fit in the overhead bin.

He wasn't quite sure what it meant that Jacey Tremblay had arrived with a full-size suitcase.

Though he was pretty sure it wasn't good.

Jacey drew in a deep breath as her eyes adjusted to the murky light inside the house. It did not smell good. Not dirty, exactly, but stale. Stuffy.

She quickly turned her attention from Trevor. She looked beyond his state of undress—difficult as that was—and the lack of warmth in his greeting, to realize he looked haggard, and her heart went out to him.

Now, two years later, it was evident from how Caitlyn's space looked and smelled that he had used up every single ounce of his considerable strength in those last weeks with his wife.

But she had seen this man tested beyond the limits of what any person should endure, and so she had a sense of *knowing* what this man was capable of.

Bravery.

Depth.

Selflessness.

Despite the current state of the house, Jacey had a sense of homecoming. She had spent so much time here, and the mark of Caitlyn's beautiful spirit remained.

It was really more a mansion than a house, like you might see in a movie or a magazine article.

The architectural style was a sophisticated

blend of modern and traditional. The main floor was open concept, the sightline going all the way from the front door to the back of the house. Huge floor-to-ceiling windows were at both ends of the space. Usually, dazzling light spilled in through those front windows that faced the lake. Now they were covered in heavy drapes that were closed against the brilliant midmorning sunlight that danced off the snow outside.

Caitlyn had somehow managed to make the cavernous space homey and welcoming with her unexpected use of color and texture. A turquoise sectional sofa and pink accent chairs—how had she managed those particular colors with Trevor?—had made the soaring Brazilian stone fireplace the focal point of the room.

The living room transitioned seamlessly to a dining room with a ten-foot harvest plank table, rescued from a two-hundred-year-old farmhouse. The table sat twenty people, easily. And had. Often.

Beyond that was the kitchen, its modern lines in sharp and lovely contrast to the old table. It had clean white lower cabinets, no uppers, lots of marble and stainless steel. There was that surprising pop of pink again in the upholstered chairs at the island and more soaring windows that should have looked out to a pool and grilling area.

But today the shutters had been closed on those windows, also.

The space had always been faintly scented of carnations, a flower Caitlyn had adored and Trevor had indulged her with several times a week; more, once she'd gotten ill.

The house had always been so glorious, luxurious but also young and fun and filled with energy, a reflection of Caitlyn's perfect life.

Now it was a testament to how temporary everything was. The front area had been reduced to a messy bachelor pad, full of pizza cartons and socks on the floor. That might even be men's underwear… Jacey carefully averted her eyes.

To the television sets. Three of them! One was on the fireplace, above the mantel, and the other two extended out from either side of it on ugly, obviously adjustable arms. There were also tangles of electrical cords.

The televisions had replaced Caitlyn's collection of gorgeous black-and-white wedding photos that had once been on, and beside, the fireplace, gallery style. Amongst the pizza boxes, on the slab of pure mango that served as a coffee table, were several very dead plants, game sleeves and controllers.

The worn boards of the harvest table were littered with papers, the magnificent Koa wood bowl, brought back from Trevor and Caitlyn's honeymoon in Hawaii, barely visible for the debris that surrounded it. The kitchen island was likewise covered with leaning stacks of dishes and smudged glasses.

Jacey could feel Trevor's presence behind her, and she turned and looked at him. His expression dared her to comment on what day it was, the state of the house, the missing photos, the dead plants, the air of neglect.

As she gazed at him, it seemed impossible that someone could look as horrible as he did, and still look so damn good at the very same time.

Not that she was looking at Trevor like *that*. Of course she wasn't!

She was just noticing the changes in him. The Trevor of two years ago had been impeccably groomed, even on the worst of days, keeping up that illusion that he wasn't falling apart as an act of love for Caitlyn. Trying to make everything easier for her.

Now Trevor's hair, a shade darker than the darkest of chocolates, was too long, the curls gloriously thick and entirely uncombed. Amongst those curls, a wild rooster tail had separated itself and was sticking straight up on the back of the crown of his head. She told herself it was only because she cared about him—the widower of her best friend—that she felt a sudden desire to smooth it down with her fingers.

Black stubble roughened the planes of high cheeks and the perfect cleft of his chin. It made him look roguish, not at all like the ultra-successful businessman he was.

Letter or no letter, Jacey was confused. She probably should not have come. He didn't want her here; that much was obvious.

Well, too bad. She didn't want to be here, either. It all felt too rife with complications, not the least of them being that she found his bristling presence awkwardly attractive.

And if it wasn't for the look in those deep brown eyes—so filled with pain, so hopeless, so empty—she might have backed out; she might have silently told Caitlyn, *I tried.*

But she knew she hadn't yet, not really, so instead of leaving, Jacey took a deep breath and folded her arms over her chest in what she hoped was a stance that portrayed firmness. Someone who did not back down.

Which was kind of laughable, but he didn't have to know that.

"Go put on a shirt," she told him. "You look like one of those guys on those calendars."

He obviously was not accustomed—at all—to being told what to do, particularly by an unexpected and uninvited visitor to his own house. Well, she was not accustomed to telling people what to do, but she was here now.

Still, Trevor's features took on an obstinate look—lowered brows, mouth set in an even firmer line. It could intimidate her, if she let it.

"What calendars?"

His bafflement seemed genuine.

She sighed. "You know. The chest-bared fireman holding the Dalmatian puppy? With the funds from sales going to the Burn Unit at the local hospital?"

He was looking at her way too closely and with faint derision as if he *knew* all about her secret stash of the kind of calendars that made a normally perfectly rational woman feel as if she might melt with longing.

"Look," Trevor said, and moved toward the door as if he intended to hold it open for her. "I know you think you're doing a good thing, and that we can prop each other up for this second anniversary. But you're mistaken. A phone call, like last year, would have sufficed."

There was no point reminding him, again, that he hadn't been answering his phone.

"I'm sorry you came all this way for nothing. I don't want to be with anybody."

And there was Jacey's excuse for the perfect exit.

CHAPTER TWO

THE EXPRESSION ON Trevor's face was steely and immovable. Despite having come a long way, Jacey felt it would be so much easier to waltz back out that door than to stay.

She could get Trevor to call her a cab, go back to the airport, grab something to eat—she realized she was starving, the subliminal message of all those pizza boxes?—and be back in her pajamas on her lovely new sofa by bedtime.

It was really what she did best—retreated, instead of standing her ground.

Except, of course, there was the letter. And her sense of duty to Caitlyn.

The easy thing was not, unfortunately, always the right thing. Was that a quote directly from her father?

Jacey had never been able to do the right thing by him, not even as motivated as she was by her need for his approval.

She shook that off.

"I don't really want to be with anyone, either,"

Jacey told him, forcing her tone to be brave. "I'm quite capable—as are you—of nursing the pain of my loss, and my bewilderment at the cruel caprice of life, all by myself."

He raised a surprised eyebrow at her agreement with him, and his hand found the doorknob and turned it.

But instead of moving toward it, as tempting as that was, Jacey went farther into this cave, slid a pizza box off the turquoise couch and sank warily onto the seat, avoiding what might have been a grease stain. The aroma was intriguing and not at all repulsive, as she would have expected it to be. Old pizza mingled with pure man.

"It's not that simple," she said, and channeled some assertiveness—probably Caitlyn's because Jacey didn't usually have any. "Go put on a shirt and then we'll talk."

Trevor looked surprised at her tone, but after a moment's consideration, left the room. That should have given Jacey plenty of time to compose herself for his return. Instead, she got up restlessly and went and opened the heavy front curtains. Light, made more brilliant by the mounds of undisturbed snow it reflected off, poured through the windows.

The view was stunning: the lake and the ice sculptures, and beyond that the swell and roll of the snowy foothills bordered by the majestic peaks of the Rocky Mountains. On a sunny day like this, the mountains looked deceptively close, as if a good brisk walk would take you there in an hour or so. On her first visit to Calgary after Caitlyn had become engaged to Trevor and moved there, Jacey had actually suggested a walk to those mountains might make a refreshing start to the day!

She had been shocked to discover that, in fact, those looming peaks were over an hour's drive away. It would take days to walk to them.

Though Jacey knew she shouldn't be so presumptuous and should leave Trevor to his obvious preference of darkness, she could not resist going and opening the back shutters, as well.

The yard was not quite as magazine-photoshoot worthy as it had been the summer the housewarming had been held there.

The pool was covered with snow, the rocky waterfall at one end of it shut off. The hot tub looked as if it had been drained of water. The outdoor kitchen was covered, and the area under the pagoda was empty of the deep, comfy yard furniture that had been there in the past.

Still, she could remember the laughter and how carefree they had all been as that summer day had melted into night. It felt as if it had been a long time since she had either laughed or been carefree.

"What have you done?"

The growl behind her made her whirl.

Trevor had been roguish before. Now, possibly because of the better light, he looked even more fabulous his hair even curlier, damp from the shower he'd obviously just taken, and his face freshly shaved. Sadly, the shirt he now wore did nothing to obliterate the memory of how he had looked shirtless. A pair of worn jeans clung to the muscles of his thighs and an aroma, clean and tingling, swept into the room with him.

She didn't like this *awareness* of him. Of course, she was aware he was attractive—how could any woman not be aware of that?—but her awareness had always been in the hands-off kind of way reserved for your best friend's husband.

And it would stay that way!

It would be easy to react to his disapproval and close the shutters again, but she didn't. Instead, Jacey lifted her chin. "I let some sun in. It's amazing out there and the views are too beautiful to be missed."

"It hurts my eyes," he said, shading his eyes dramatically.

"There's no need to act as if you're a vampire who can be slayed by light."

"I like it dark in here."

"That is obvious."

He looked around, and his mouth turned downward in an aggravated line at how the light illuminated the mess. "It makes it easier to ignore dust. And other, er, debris. It's also better for the television screens."

Okay, so she had probably overstepped herself opening the drapes.

Still, that explanation for the darkness he was living in told her far more than he had intended.

This was why Caitlyn had sent her. This man—Caitlyn's beloved husband—was, even after two years, behaving like a wounded bear, blocking out everything from his life, even the sun. Distracting himself from his pain.

One thing Jacey needed to remember: wounded bears were extremely dangerous. Actually, there were probably two things she needed to remember: wounded bears were extremely dangerous, and she was the least likely person to ever confront one.

"Tell me why you're here," he said, his voice gravelly with menace and pain.

Since he wasn't going to invite her, Jacey gathered her courage and went past him, back into the living room, and took up her seat on the sofa. He followed her, threw himself into one of the pink chairs opposite her, hooked one long leg over the arm of it and gave her a look that was impatient at best and irritated at worst. It was hard to ignore the fact that his masculinity was in no way threatened by the color of the chair.

"Please don't keep me in suspense. Why are you here?"

"Caitlyn wrote me a letter," she said quietly.

The grim lines around his mouth deepened. His brows lowered ferociously as he bit out a few words. "Where Caitlyn is, you don't write letters."

"Believe me, it was an unexpected surprise. I just got it a few days ago. She must have left instructions with a lawyer. To time it for...you know."

Oh, he knew. She saw the shock—and hurt—register in his face.

"She wrote *you* a letter," he said flatly.

"I think she wrote it to me because if she wrote it to you, what are the chances you would be sitting in Toronto on my sofa right now?"

Jacey suddenly wondered if Trevor would like her sofa, which was absolute madness. But of course, the whole mission was absolute madness.

Thanks, Caitlyn.

"How did you react to the pink chairs?" Jacey heard herself asking. "When they first came home?"

Trevor looked bewildered, as well he should, by the unexpected change of subject. It was absurd how badly she, fresh from a relationship where she had never bought a single piece of furniture she liked for fear of disapproval, needed to know.

He looked at the arm of the chair his leg was draped over. Something in his expression softened.

"I hated them," he said, gruffly. "I hated these

chairs so much. But I looked at her face when she was showing them to me, and she was just glowing with excitement. She wanted so badly for me to like them. And then it was weird. I just did like them. Not pretending or anything. I just liked them because of what they did to her."

Some emotion clawed horribly at Jacey's throat, his statement making her painfully aware of the deficiencies in her own marriage. This is what she had missed. Love—wanting the other person's happiness more than your own—trumping the color of furniture.

Trevor looked annoyed with himself then, as if he had revealed a state secret.

"Okay," he said, rolling his shoulders, shaking it off. "So Caitlyn wrote you a letter. Why?"

Jacey took a deep breath. "The letter said she doesn't want us—you and me—to be sitting around moping our lives away."

He winced and looked away.

"She knew us, Trevor," Jacey said quietly, trying to convey the love she had felt in that letter—and had just seen again in the story of the pink chairs. That story made her feel more committed to this rescue than she had been at any moment since she had opened the package.

"She knew we'd just stop living."

"I'm living," he said, but Jacey was heartbroken by the regret she heard in his voice, as if he didn't really care to be alive at all.

"I don't think she meant just going through the motions of living," Jacey said carefully. "I think she guessed we'd be living without joy. Without having fun."

"I'm having fun. Three television sets and a steady diet of pizza. Are you kidding me? I can watch three separate sporting events at once. Livin' the dream here." His tone was flat and he squinted at her, daring her to argue.

"What I'm trying to say," Jacey said, weighing her words even more carefully, "is that Caitlyn knew that, left to our own devices, both of us would just sink into a mess of morass, and without a little push we might just stay there."

"That's ridiculous," Trevor said, but he slid a look around the mess his house was in, now harshly illuminated by the light pouring in the windows. The realization crossed his face that morass probably described his circumstances just about perfectly.

"Anyway," he said, "what does she want us to do? It's been two years and I still don't know how to move on. If I knew how to do that, wouldn't I have done it already?"

His pain was so intense, just as his love for Caitlyn had been.

"Why don't you look at what she sent me?" Jacey suggested.

She got up, deposited the letter on his lap and went and sat back down on the couch, facing him. She watched Trevor's face as he unfolded the piece of paper.

There was unguarded softness as he recognized the handwriting, followed by growing hardness. Once done, he set the letter down and ran a hand through the silk of his still-wet hair. It made that rooster tail pop up. He pulled in a deep breath and then fixed Jacey with a look.

"She knew we might be sad, and get stuck there," Jacey told him, then finished softly, "She just wants us to be okay."

"Well, that's not possible," he said. "To be *okay.*"

She passed him the second envelope. "I don't think we need to look at it as moving on," she suggested softly, "so much as somehow rediscovering that joy for life she gave us. That she gave everything she did."

Trevor gave her a dark, pained look, then let the contents of the envelope spill out onto his lap. He filtered through them, picking up one item, glancing at it and casting it away to go on to the next. The entire time his expression darkened.

"No," he finally said.

Really, it was exactly what she had expected. Hadn't that been her initial reaction, as well?

"Okay," Jacey said, mostly relieved, though maybe a teeny-tiny bit disappointed. Like 99 percent to 1 percent.

"A ski excursion?" Trevor snorted derisively.

"Moonbeam Peaks for three days? Not even maybe."

"Okay," she said again, conciliatorily.

"Caitlyn and I met on a ski hill."

"I know," Jacey said, and then went on, despite the fierce expression on Trevor's face. "I remember her telling me the worst possible thing had happened. That she'd fallen for a ski bum."

She was rewarded when the most reluctant smile tugged at the firm line of his lips.

"Our first fight," Trevor remembered, "was when she found out I wasn't a ski bum. Imagine that. Angry because I was a gainfully employed engineer."

"That's a bit of an understatement. You weren't just a gainfully employed engineer. You were some kind of fabulously well-known—not to mention rich—tycoon."

"Now, that's a bit of an overstatement. I'd made a name for myself. I am *not*, by any stretch of the imagination, a tycoon."

"Do you prefer *billionaire*?" she asked sweetly.

He scowled at her but made no denial.

"Anyway, Caitlyn wasn't angry with you because you were fabulously rich and famous. She was angry because you lied to her."

He was silent for a moment. "Did you discuss it?"

"Of course!"

He mulled that over, then sighed.

"It was after that fight that I knew I was going to marry her," he said, his tone pensive. "Because she loved me *before* she knew. It was just such a novelty being liked for who I was, not for what I had. I did play the broke ski bum for far too long. But I convinced her to forgive me."

"You did," Jacey said.

"I don't think I can ski. Ever again. Why would she even ask that of me?"

"She knew your greatest joy was on the slopes."

"My greatest joy was her, Jacey."

Jacey tried to hold it together. She really did. But today marked two years since she had lost her best friend. Plus, his words were like a sword that pierced her own sense of failure and disillusionment over the dissolution of her marriage.

To be *that*. Someone's greatest joy.

She was so glad Caitlyn had experienced it. And so, so sad that her best friend and Trevor had not had the happy ending they so richly deserved.

Her lip trembled. She could feel her eyes stinging and her throat aching.

She glanced at Trevor. He looked terrified that she was going to start crying.

Do not cry, she ordered herself. *Do not.*

He swore under his breath. He closed his eyes. He folded his hands over his belly. He opened one eye and slid her a pleading look before closing it again.

"Please don't," he whispered.

"I'm trying not to."

"Good."

She bit down hard on the inside of her cheek and swallowed twice. Thankfully, it worked.

"I'm okay now," she said, her voice only a tiny bit wobbly.

"I'm not going to go spend three days at Moonbeam Peaks," he repeated with careful patience, but steely resolve.

Moonbeam Peaks was a very famous ski village just outside the Rocky Mountain township of Banff, a town at the very entrance to those Rocky Mountains they could see out his front window.

He opened his eyes and glanced at the cards and papers and tickets that had spilled out of the envelope onto his lap.

He picked up one and glared at it. He waved a voucher at her. "I'm especially not going tomorrow. I have a life."

His life—the televisions and game stations laid out in front of them—seemed to mock that statement, a fact of which he seemed aware since he fixed her with a defensive glare.

"I'm not going tomorrow, either," Jacey decided, relieved. "I have a life, too."

CHAPTER THREE

JACEY CONSIDERED THAT. *I have a life, too.* It was almost as bad a lie as Trevor telling Caitlyn he was a ski bum.

Because right now her life consisted of a failed marriage.

And a failed career.

Her life to-do list included getting an application form that could lead her to a bright new career as a checkout cashier at Grab-n-Go. She'd probably make more money.

But she certainly wasn't going to get into all that with Trevor Cooper, billionaire extraordinaire!

And there was absolutely no reason to admit she actually had cleared her "life" schedule—and bought new pajamas—to do exactly as Caitlyn had suspected she would do: wallow in the pit of her despair in the days leading up to, and following, the tragic anniversary.

"I'm not going tomorrow or any other day," Trevor said as if she might have felt he had left himself open to negotiation. "Geez. Two years are up. Did she think there's a magical line on the calendar? One day you feel this way. The next you don't. Let's go skiing."

"I know it's crazy. I knew from the moment I opened the envelope how crazy it was. I mean, I don't even know how to ski," Jacey agreed.

Still, hadn't part of her leaned, just a little bit, toward Caitlyn's plan? Because it was insane in that delightful Caitlyn way that was the antithesis of the Jacey way. Caitlyn's way was spontaneity, unexpected adventures, pure delight for life.

In her careful world, Jacey missed her friend's influence so much.

It occurred to her that getting on that airplane today had been the first spontaneous thing she had done since Caitlyn had died. Unless the purchase of the love seat counted.

But she would have to concede defeat. Her efforts would have to be good enough. Trevor had read the letter; he'd looked at the trip and activities that Caitlyn had planned, and he'd said *no*.

Caitlyn, of all people, should have known Jacey was not the best person for this job. Convincing Trevor to do something he didn't want to do would require someone more assertive than Jacey knew herself to be. Maybe even pushy.

The silence stretched between them. He broke it.

"Why did you come all this way if you didn't

want to go? You must have known I wouldn't go. You could have just called."

"Yes, you've already suggested that. You're not answering your phone," she reminded him.

"Oh, yeah," he said, "there is that."

"The airline ticket, Toronto to Calgary, was in the packet, in my name, with this date on it. I tried to do what I thought she wanted done."

Why *had* she come all this way when she had suspected, from the moment she had looked at the contents of that envelope, that it was pretty much mission impossible? She was not known for being impulsive! She was known for being careful, measured. Maybe even hesitant. No, definitely hesitant.

"I had to," Jacey admitted, puzzling through it as she spoke. "I had to bring her message. I had to know I had done everything I could do to deliver it, to do what she wanted me to do and exactly the way she wanted me to do it."

He grunted as if he got it. Just a little bit. It was a tiny encouragement, but it did help her muster her bravery.

"It *was* her dying wish," Jacey ventured, after a while.

"I think she had to make that wish *before* she died in order to plan it," he said. His voice was like ice, and yet right underneath that, Jacey could hear a veritable mountain of pain.

"I guess *technically* it would have been made

before she died," Jacey said, carefully. "She would have had to contact lawyers, tell them what she wanted and when. I'm assuming they looked after the details."

Trevor suddenly fixed her with a look.

"What does your husband think of all this?"

Trevor noticed Jacey was suddenly looking everywhere but at him. There were lots of things for her to look at. Was that a pair of his underwear on the floor? Her eyes skittered past that and she pretended sudden interest in the golf game unfolding on screen number three.

He reached for the remote and shut off all three televisions.

"I'm sorry," he said. "His name escapes me."

"Bruce," she squeaked.

"You're not together, are you?" he asked her softly.

She hesitated, then tilted her chin and held up her empty ring finger. "Divorced," she said. "Finally."

He was not the least bit fooled by her attempt at a cavalier tone. If ever a girl wasn't the *I'm happily divorced* type it was her.

Of course, if ever a man wasn't the *I'm a widower* type it was him. And yet, here he was. Life was full of nasty surprises. Why did that continue to surprise him?

"I'm sorry," Trevor said. The thing was he *really* was.

Jacey lifted a shoulder. While he had showered and dressed, she'd lost the jacket, and he noticed how painfully thin she was. She was dressed practically, for travel, in wrinkle-free dark trousers and a plain white button-up shirt.

This is what he remembered about her, with deep gratitude. That she was practical. Jacey was that quiet force in the background making things happen.

"Wow," he said, "tough couple of years."

It occurred to him, just on the periphery of his being, that he *cared* about her suffering. It was a first. Caring about anything other than his own pain. He was not sure he welcomed it.

"What happened?" he asked. He remembered Jacey's wedding, maybe a year after his and Caitlyn's. Caitlyn had been in Jacey's bridal party, just as Jacey had been in hers.

It had been a small, budget-friendly event. Jacey, who seemed to cultivate an air of the unremarkable, he recalled now, had been the most remarkable thing about that day: her then long, blond hair piled up on her head and threaded with ribbons; her features expertly made up to show how delicate and perfect they were.

He recalled her eyes, huge and green, brimming with joy and hope for the future. It felt like a knife jab remembering those days when they had all been so filled with optimism. They hadn't been particularly young and yet, looking back, it seemed they had been very young. Hopelessly naive.

Planning their house purchases and vacations and career successes—and children, especially children—as if they truly believed nothing bad could ever happen to them.

Jacey hesitated. "Obviously, my relationship with Bruce had a few cracks in it. When pressure was applied…it went *kaboom*."

She flung out her hands with the *kaboom*, signaling a world being blown to smithereens.

"What pressure?" Trevor asked.

She was silent.

"Tell me," Trevor said. Why did he feel like he needed to know so badly what, beyond death, shattered dreams? It felt as if he wanted to know so that he could build the bastions of disillusionment even higher around himself.

"When Caitlyn got sick, I had to come here for her. Bruce didn't get it. We'd just bought a house." She made a strangled sound that might have been an attempt at a laugh. "Probably one we couldn't really afford. We needed both our incomes to make the payment."

Trevor felt stunned to learn of the sacrifice Jacey had made. In all the time she had spent with them leading up to Caitlyn's death, she had never said a single word about it.

"Why wouldn't you tell me that?" he asked sharply. "I could have asked my mom to come more. Or Caitlyn's."

"Oh, Trevor," she said softly, and with faint reprimand that reminded him how hard this had been on the two mothers, his and Caitlyn's, both of them shattered and frail.

"I would have helped you with your payments," he snapped, with more irritation than he intended. "It's the least I could have done."

She gave him the kind of sad look he remembered sometimes Caitlyn would give him. It meant: *You're not as smart as you think you are.*

"My father used to say that any kind of problem that could be solved with money wasn't really a problem," she told him softly.

Somewhere in the back of his mind, he recalled Caitlyn telling him Jacey had been raised by a single dad. There had been something else his wife had said about the relationship, but he couldn't remember what it was. Was it that they'd been poor? It sounded like the kind of statement someone without money made.

Still, regardless of the motivation for the statement, there was an undeniable truth to it and one he was well aware of. Caitlyn's death being a case in point. All the money in the world could not save her, had left him reeling in the truth that in a world where money was generally regarded as power, a man could still be powerless.

"You never said anything," Trevor said, appalled. What would he have done if he knew she was going to lose her husband and her home to be there with them?

She smiled shakily, her eyes looking huge and suspiciously damp. Was he going to have to beg her not to cry again?

"There was no way I would say anything. Add to your and Caitlyn's burdens?"

"I could have given you the money," he said stubbornly.

"But could you have given me a man that understood the importance of loyalty, the honor of being there for a friend, the absolute grace of serving with love?"

Trevor saw, then, exactly who Jacey was. He was shaken, not just by the truth he saw in her, but in the truth that was revealed about himself.

It was not a comfortable truth.

"I think maybe Caitlyn knew your marriage was in trouble," Trevor said slowly.

"I hope she didn't. I tried not to let on."

But his wife had become almost spookily intuitive in those last months and especially in the final weeks of her life. He remembered the worried look on her face after Jacey would come in from a phone call with Bruce, the way her eyes followed her friend, soft with sympathy. Even dying, Caitlyn was able to put her own difficulties aside and *see*.

Caitlyn had known what Jacey was giving up for her. No, for *them*.

Trevor was not sure how he would have gotten through those final days without Jacey in the background. Making sure he ate. Giving him clean clothes. Being a calm presence in a chaotic, constantly unfolding situation.

Jacey had been there, loving Caitlyn, when he needed to grab a few hours of sleep, or walk away from the intensity of it all, just for a few minutes or hours.

Jacey had been there, after, for all the difficult phone calls and the hard arrangements.

She had even protected his mother, Jane, and his mother-in-law, Mary, sending them away when she saw it was too much for them, that they were being overwhelmed.

He might not have realized at the time just how much they needed protecting, but a few months ago both had arrived and quietly cleaned his house and cleared away Caitlyn's clothing and personal items. Thinking it would help him.

It had nearly killed them both.

Watching her stuff being boxed up had nearly had the same effect on him.

Trevor saw, suddenly, that Caitlyn's last wish wasn't for him.

It was a way of trying to thank the friend who had given up everything for her. For them. What had Caitlyn said about Jacey?

That she had no idea how mighty she was.

But hadn't he seen her bravery? Hadn't he seen her mightiness on a daily basis? Jacey, who had even protected the two mothers from so much of the burden, who had taken all of it on her slender shoulders.

And even if the last wish wasn't for him, the last message was.

Trevor, be a better man.

He let the feeling of shame come. His defensiveness, his pain, had allowed him to be rude to Jacey, to not welcome her in the way she deserved to be welcomed. So what if today was a hard day?

Be a better man.

He saw he had missed his opportunity to beg her not to cry. She was biting down hard on the plumpness of her lower lip, but a single tear slipped from her eye and slid down her cheek. She wiped it away hastily. But it was followed by another. And then another.

Be a better man.

Trevor got up from his chair. He went and sat beside her. Awkwardly, he took her hand. It was warm and soft in his. She gripped him as if he had thrown her a lifeline. He was acutely aware of how, for two whole years, he had avoided human contact, fraught as it was with the potential for pain.

"I'm sorry," he said again, his voice rough with his own held-in emotions.

Unfortunately, it made the tears come harder and faster. She made a little hiccupping noise. And then, still with her hand gripping his, she turned her face into his chest and just sobbed.

"Two years without her," she whispered. "The world feels so different now. I miss her so much."

It was the way he wanted to sob. The way he had wanted to every single day since he had kissed Caitlyn goodbye for the very last time.

"It's okay," he said awkwardly, patting her back, his clumsiness making him aware he was out of practice at these rituals of human connection. "There, there, it's okay."

It wasn't really. As Jacey's scent, clean and lemony, tickled his nostrils, and her tears pooled into a warm puddle on his chest, he knew that. He knew it never would be okay again.

But he also knew, in the name of being the man his wife had always believed he was, he was going to be going to Moonbeam Peaks for the next few days.

"I can't believe you've never skied," he said to her, putting Jacey away from him, taking his hand from hers and holding her shoulders in what? A nice, brotherly gesture of support?

"You can live without having skied," she said, trying to smile through the tears.

"Not once you've done it, you can't." With someone else, he might have added, jokingly, *like an orgasm*, but he bit his tongue before he said that to Jacey.

He considered the jokingly part. How long since he had joked around?

And just a minute ago he had said he would never ski again. Whether he wanted it to or not, his life seemed to already be changing in subtle ways now that Jacey was here, and Caitlyn's final wish had been revealed.

And yet, with that realization he felt, not defeat, but a sudden unexpected swoop of anticipation at the thought of the slopes, the skis, the snow, introducing someone else to that magical world.

Maybe those slopes would even reveal Jacey's mightiness to her.

For an astounding moment Trevor felt exactly what he had vowed he would never feel again.

Alive.

It was a reminder that his wife's well-meaning wish for her friend—and for him—was putting him on very dangerous ground.

He was aware Caitlyn might have approved of the uneasy feelings her last request was causing in him.

Trevor got up abruptly and moved away from Jacey, trying to clear his head. It was hard to do with her tears still wetting the front of his shirt. He was extraordinarily annoyed with himself. For *feeling*. For giving in.

For that speck of happy anticipation he had felt when he'd given in.

Jacey's suitcase was still in the middle of the floor. It was wildly neon, with a pattern in pinks and greens, as if it was revealing a secret personality that was not in keeping with the Jacey he knew: responsible, reliable, calm, brimming with common sense, low-key.

The suitcase said she was mighty. Bold.

The fact that she had committed to coming across the country on the basis of a letter might also be a hint that there were facets of her he was unaware of. That she hid, even from herself.

"I bought it to come," she said as if she needed to defend herself against the bright choice of the suitcase. "I wanted one that I could pick out easily at the luggage carousel."

"Okay," he said, running a hand through his hair. "Let's figure this thing out. Do you have what you need for a few days in the mountains?"

CHAPTER FOUR

"OH, ABSOLUTELY," JACEY SAID.

Trevor's doubt must have shown in his face.

"Three days, three books."

"For a ski vacation?"

"I figured the ski part of the package was for you. I was thinking a comfy chair by a fireplace and good books for me. But I packed mittens! You know, in case I venture outside."

Mittens, Trevor thought incredulously. Who went to a ski resort and *maybe ventured* outside? Whether Jacey knew it or not, she needed to ski. He saw, suddenly, what a perfect gift this had been to her from her friend.

And being there with her, lending his expertise, was what he was agreeing to take on: an essential part of the being-a-better-man equation.

"Do you have a different coat?" he asked. "A different one from the one you were wearing when you arrived at my door?" *When you turned my whole world upside down in the space of seconds?*

"Well, no, I thought with a sweater I could make do with the one I have. I packed two sweaters," she said brightly.

It was apparent Jacey was hopelessly unprepared for a mountain excursion, even of the most civilized variety, Trevor thought. He began a mental list: *ski jacket.*

"I guess ski pants are out of the question?" he asked her.

"Ski pants? I told you I won't need those for sipping hot chocolate in the lounge while *you* ski. That's what Caitlyn's wish was. For you to ski."

Trevor, however, was pretty certain his wife's wish was for him to focus on Jacey's enjoyment. And if she had never skied, he was going to make sure she did that.

"Are you familiar at all with Moonbeam?" he asked.

"No."

"Ah."

"Why do you say it like that?"

"There's no road up to the village. There's only one way to arrive at the resort and that's by gondola. There are a few shops at the ski village, but it's probably a good idea to arrive with at least the basics."

"Gondola," she repeated, her eyes wide. She giggled nervously. "I take it you don't mean the nice kind. Like in Italy."

"Italy?"

"Venice? Boats? Man standing? Singing?"

What was she talking about?

She sang a few bars, "Figaro, Figaro."

"Geez, no, not that kind. Obviously. The cable car type. But they're really nice. Completely enclosed from the weather. Comfy. Spectacular views."

"To be honest, I've never been very good at heights."

"It's an experience you really can't miss," he said.

"Like skiing?" she asked.

And orgasms. Where was that coming from? It had to stop. You didn't have thoughts like that anywhere in the vicinity of your wife's best friend. There were unwritten rules about these things.

"It seems maybe I've missed a few of life's essential experiences." Her tone was chipper, but she looked worried.

Step one to uncovering her bold and mighty side, he thought, would be getting her on the gondola. Since the very idea had made her go quite pale, even while she was trying to joke about Venice gondolas, Trevor thought this might be a bigger challenge than his wife had anticipated.

"You can do it," he assured her.

"I guess I have to try," she said uncertainly.

"There will be a rental shop up there for skis," he said, thinking out loud, moving on to try to take her mind off her gondola trepidation.

"I haven't exactly committed to the skiing idea! I'll need to recuperate from the gondola."

"You could try boarding. Whatever you prefer." He read her blank expression. She really wasn't even aware there was a difference between skiing and snowboarding.

"There will be lots to occupy me while you ski."

It occurred to him this excursion was going to be a huge undertaking, probably beginning with convincing her to get on the gondola and then to use the slopes.

"Look," he said, "I'll bring your suitcase upstairs. You might as well plan on staying here tonight and we'll leave first thing in the morning."

It felt familiar to be making a plan.

Taking charge.

Not good, exactly, but edging toward normal.

"You can go through your suitcase and separate anything you think might be useful for a ski holiday—"

"A reading-in-front-of-the-fire holiday," she corrected him. "After surviving a ride in a gondola."

"Millions of other people have survived the gondola. You'll be fine. Then let's assume," he said, and heard the dryness in his own voice, "that you might put your nose outside once in three days."

She beamed at him. "I brought mittens, just to address that very possibility!"

"Well, yippee. Of course, that's assuming they're the right kind."

"The right kind? Of mittens?"

"You don't want anything that absorbs moisture, so cute woolies are out."

He could tell from the disgruntled look on her face exactly the kind of mittens that were tucked inside that suitcase.

"That's if you're planning on getting wet!"

He sighed. "Can we assume you might throw a snowball? Participate in some *snowy* activity at a *mountain resort*?"

"I'm not planning on it," she said with a hint of stubbornness.

"Here's something you and I both know," he told her, softly, sternly. "Life doesn't always go according to plan. Just lay out your stuff for me and I'll decide if it really is useful or not. Meanwhile, I'll go through that envelope and see exactly what Caitlyn had in mind for the next few days so we can be properly prepared."

To cut off any further argument from her, he hauled her suitcase upstairs and put her in the guest room. She was already familiar with it, so he wouldn't need to tell her where anything was.

She followed him up and shut the door behind her with just a little more snap than might have been strictly necessary.

He went back downstairs and heard the shower turn on as he gathered all the items from the envelope Jacey had brought and took them to his kitchen island.

There was a woman showering in his house. It had been a long, long time since life had surprised him like this, but since the moment Jacey had arrived an element of the unpredictable had shivered in the air.

Focus, he ordered himself. He swept the existing clutter down to one end of the island, and then began to organize the items from the envelope Caitlyn had sent.

Trevor realized, unwanted surprises aside, he was, for the first time in two years, a man with a mission.

That mission, Trevor told himself, was to put the needs of another human being ahead of his own. To take care of Jacey. To help her break out from under the shadow of grief and give her a few moments of fun.

Real fun. Not sitting in front of the fireplace with a book.

His mission was to help her discover her mightiness.

He was suddenly aware he had not offered her a single thing to eat or drink after her long trip. Mightiness probably needed nourishment!

"Are you hungry?" he called up to her when he heard the shower turn off.

"Famished," she called back.

"Why don't I order something? Do you have any preferences?"

"I seem to have a sudden craving for pizza."

He actually laughed. He heard it, rusty in his throat. "A girl after my own heart," he said.

And then wondered if it was okay to say that.

This was a brand-new world, with brand-new rules, that he was navigating with his wife's best friend. It felt oddly complicated.

He called for a pizza and then focused intently on the contents of that envelope, sorting them into piles that brought order, his favorite thing, not that you would know it right now from the state of his house.

Most of the items were in the form of vouchers.

Hotel accommodations for two nights.

Lesson reservations. For one person.

Ski passes, for two people, for three days. Caitlyn, apparently, was with him on this: Jacey was not to spend three days reading books in front of the fire.

His wife did not want her best friend to be alone this week, and he could dig deep inside himself to make sure that her wishes were carried out.

Jacey arrived downstairs just as he completed making an agenda and a list of basics they would need for her. He folded that and put it in his pocket. He could cross off items if she had brought anything that was appropriate.

Which he highly doubted.

He slid her a look. Considering how hard she seemed to work at appearing unremarkable, he could see she was lovely, in that understated way of true beauty: no makeup, no fussing with her hair, or her wardrobe.

Her hair was spiky from being towel dried. A fragrance, soapy and clean, wafted off her and she had changed into yoga pants and a dark T-shirt.

Her eyes looked huge—possibly because she was so thin. Still, it was her eyes that gave him a glimpse of the real her: that strong spirit, rooted in an old-fashioned ability to be compassionate, to serve, to love deeply and unconditionally.

The mission, he reminded himself sternly, was straightforward. Three days of introducing Jacey to the joy of the mountains, and therefore, to herself.

Three days of being a better man.

It was completely doable.

The pizza arrived and she cleared a space at the dining table. Because she had spent time here, she knew where everything was and she went and got plates and cutlery and napkins. It had been a long time since he had eaten at this table or put out a plate. These were simple things, and yet, it felt again, as if *normal* was crowding at him, and he wasn't ready for it.

He could do it for three days.

He opened the lid of the pizza box and put a piece on her plate for her. They had done this so many times when Caitlyn was ill. Sat at this table, heart-weary and broken, eating takeout, talking in quiet voices about their day, what needed to be done next.

But oddly, sitting here with her again, those didn't feel like bad memories. It just felt right to have Jacey here, in a space that seemed to belong to both of them.

The next morning, predawn, Jacey squinted through the windshield of the SUV. She was terrified.

It was in such sharp contrast to how she had felt last night, back in that familiar bedroom, her tummy filled with pizza, a down comforter over her.

Trevor under the same roof.

She had felt content, somehow. Safe.

How quickly things could change! She tried to pick out elements of a landscape, but they were completely hidden behind a veil of darkness and heavily falling snow.

"This reminds me of a ride I was on once at an amusement park," she said as the white particles of snow caught and glittered in the narrow tunnel of the headlamps, swirled, smashed on the windshield and were swept away.

"Yeah," Trevor said, "it's kind of fun, isn't it?"

Fun? If this was his idea of fun, her plan to sit inside reading for the next few days was looking like an exceedingly good one!

"That ride was extremely frightening, and so is this," she told him, grimly. "How could this happen? It was such a nice day yesterday."

"They have a saying in Alberta. If you don't like the weather, wait five minutes."

"But I did like the weather! It was gorgeous and sunny. Where did this storm come from?"

"These mountain climates are notoriously unpredictable." He cast her a look. "Are you really frightened?"

"Yes! It's my first experience with a whiteout."

"You have bad weather in Toronto. It's Canada!"

"We have the kind of bad weather in TO that makes you put on your *woolly* mittens, pull your hood over your forehead and wait for the bus *inside* the shelter. Not the kind where you could slide off a road, into the forest and be lost forever."

Did he snicker? Ever so slightly? She sent him a look. His face was impassive.

"Uh, we're not in the forest yet," he said with maddening calm. "Not even close. Rolling hills. Ranch country. The kind of place you can watch your dog run away for three hours. If we go off the road—and we aren't going to—we aren't going to disappear into a wilderness abyss."

"Quit trying to be funny. It's starting to get light out there, and I still can't see anything. It's a bona fide blizzard, isn't it?"

Her voice had a shrill note she would have controlled if she could have.

"I'm not sure I'd call it that." His voice was rich and calm, soothing, if she'd allow herself to be soothed. She considered allowing it.

"It's a bit of a winter squall," he clarified.

"What's the difference between a squall and a blizzard?" she demanded.

He cast her a look and smiled at her. He pushed a button on his dash and asked, "Hey, Jeeves, what's the difference between a squall and a blizzard?"

A robotic voice answered, "A squall is much more dangerous than a blizzard. They involve heavy bursts of snow that can result in whiteout conditions and falling temperatures that freeze road surfaces and create hazardous—"

He hastily shut off the voice.

"More dangerous than a blizzard," Jacey said woodenly.

"Hey!" Trevor said. "On the bright side, we have internet connection. See? We're not exactly heading off in a covered wagon across the uncharted wilderness."

"Just as I suspected," Jacey said, sadly, peering out into a storm that was not made any better for the fact daylight was trying to pierce the murky grayness of it. "The day has plenty of potential for catastrophe."

"As does life," he pointed out, quietly, but then with cheery determination added, "Let's keep it in perspective. It's not a tour of duty in some bug-infested hellhole where everyone is intent on killing you."

She remembered, vaguely, he'd done some time in the military before he had gone on to university, gotten a degree in engineering, become a very wealthy businessman and met Caitlyn. That would explain how damnably relaxed he was.

Yes, her own ability to ferret out catastrophe had been a part of her life ever since she had sat at a grand piano at thirteen, in front of a select audience, about to give her first concert.

She had completely frozen. Completely.

That sense of every day holding the potential for impending doom had taken another giant leap forward when her beautiful, young best friend— a woman with everything to live for—had been diagnosed with a terminal illness.

She suspected this was part of Caitlyn's motive in sending her on this excursion. She would have known that Jacey was going to do a full retreat to safety after losing her friend.

"I was born and raised in Calgary," Trevor told her.

Was his voice naturally soothing or was it de-

liberate? Either way, she could feel herself leaning into it.

"I've been driving to Banff National Park and
the ski resorts there since a week after I got my
driver's license. I've made this trip hundreds,
maybe even thousands, of times."

"Hmph," she said in defiance of the part of her
that wanted to lean in to the calm and strength
she heard in his voice.

"You know what the most dangerous thing in
the world is?" he asked her solemnly.

Oh, yeah. She knew that one.

CHAPTER FIVE

LOVE, JACEY THOUGHT. Love was the most dangerous thing in the world.

"Your bathroom," Trevor said, sagely.

That was annoying! She was thinking esoteric thoughts, and he was being aggravatingly earthbound. Still, there was a lesson in the difference between men and women, right there.

"Wow. That gives new meaning to *get your mind out of the toilet*," she noted, and then added, "Besides, that's ridiculous."

"It isn't. Slips and falls in bathrooms kill way more people annually than, say, airline crashes."

"I'm also terrified of flying."

"Somehow, I guessed," he said dryly.

"Damn. Who wants people being able to guess something like that?"

"You already told me you were scared of heights."

"Flying is a separate fear entirely." Sheesh. Just as she wanted to come off. *Timid*. But was there any hiding it? "And a legitimate one, I might add."

"Well, except for the bathroom thing."

"How would you know something like that?" Jacey, who wanted to be bold and wasn't, asked him grouchily. "That bathrooms kill more people than airline crashes?"

He nodded sagely at the dashboard. "Jeeves had made me an expert on all kinds of unlikely topics."

"Thanks, Jeeves. I'll probably never look at my bathroom in quite the same way again."

He flashed her a grin and, suddenly, there was that awareness of him again. He looked particularly attractive this morning, dressed casually in a navy blue sweater that showed off the impossible broadness of his shoulders and depth of his chest. He had on matching navy blue ski pants that hugged him in all the right places.

That crazy rooster tail was sticking up out of his chocolate curls, and her fingers itched to reach over and smooth it.

The heater was circulating warm air and his scent, and both pierced her fear like light pierced darkness. Her awareness of how attractive he was was distracting in the nicest way. Her awareness that love, not bathrooms, was the most dangerous thing in the world, felt more threatening than the raging storm.

That just felt *wrong*. To be thinking of Trevor and love in the same sentence. He was Caitlyn's.

Only, what did that mean *now*?

Stop it, Jacey told herself. If anything, Caitlyn's death and his suffering, and her own, just proved her point. Love, not bathrooms, *was* the most dangerous threat of all.

Still, what did it mean to her relationship with Trevor now that Caitlyn was gone? Did it have to mean anything? Did everything have to mean something? Did her whole life have to be a study in the seriousness of unintended consequences? Did she have to ferret out catastrophe because it had visited her in the past?

Of course not. She could consciously decide not to be timid, couldn't she? Jacey was aware she needed to accept this gift in the spirit it had been given.

Was it not possible to just relax and enjoy the unexpected adventure? Even being caught in a storm with an extremely capable guy could be interpreted as an adventure instead of a harbinger of doom, couldn't it? What was it *other* people said?

Enjoy the moment.

With effort, she forced herself to breathe.

She had taken several yoga classes online, after Caitlyn had died, hoping to find moments not filled with angst, memories, pain, powerlessness. She had taken more after the failure of her marriage and more again after Johnny's horrible, unexpected audition result.

It *had* helped.

She closed her eyes. Deep breath. Through the nose. Out the mouth. She felt the breath move like a cool wave, up through her nostrils, and down her throat. She expelled it gently.

"Are you hyperventilating?" Trevor asked, worried.

"No! I'm practicing Ujjayi."

"Is that a martial art I'm unaware of? Should I brace myself for a karate chop to the throat?"

She refused to open her eyes. "It's a breathing technique. Yoga."

"Ah, yoga," he said. Was there the tiniest hint of amusement in his voice?

"I'm not likely to karate chop you in the throat while my life is in your most capable hands."

She opened her eyes. She looked at his most capable hands, relaxed on the steering wheel. His fingers were long and strong, his wrists square and masculine. There was that *awareness* again. Maybe even something more. A longing.

Not for him—of course not for him!—but for things masculine in her purple-pansy sofa world. She quickly shut her eyes again.

Still, as she breathed, Jacey became aware that while a storm raged outside, warm air blew gently on her. The lovely, masculine, reassuring scent of Trevor was in the air. The poignant notes of a classical guitar embraced them. After a while she remembered there was a coffee in the cup holder beside her.

She opened her eyes and reached for it and took a sip. Caffeine was probably not the best answer to rattled nerves, but it tasted unbelievably good.

To her surprise her fear melted away, replaced with a lovely, languid sense of calm. Of safety. Trevor was handling the conditions with such ease. She suspected it was his confidence, as much as the Ujjayi, that was making her feel like this. Almost catlike: calm and alert at the very same time.

She tried to remember the last time she had felt this way. Peaceful. Connected. Protected, somehow.

She realized she had known Caitlyn and Trevor years, and then lived with them for weeks, and that, really, beyond the fact he had loved her best friend intensely, and that Caitlyn had returned that love, she didn't know very much about him.

"What do engineers do?" she asked. "Caitlyn was always vague about what you did for a living."

He laughed. "There's a reason for that. There are probably twenty different kinds of engineers, only one of them being in any way what most people would consider interesting. I'm a mechanical engineer, which is far more boring than my romantic cousin, the structural engineer."

Well, Jacey thought, thank goodness he wasn't the *romantic* type of engineer.

"Caitlyn's eyes glazed over when I talked about work. In fact so do most people's."

"Perfect! A nice boring topic to keep my eyes off the deepening winter conditions unfolding around us."

He chuckled, considered, gave in. "Basically, I design or improve mechanical systems used for processing and manufacturing."

"You're right," she said with a happy sigh. "Exceedingly dull."

"Ever since I was a kid," Trevor confided, "I was obsessed with taking things apart and seeing how they worked. I was quite nerdy in my formative years."

She glanced at him, felt her mouth fall open—Trevor, nerdy?—and then snapped it closed again before he registered how incredulous the thought made her.

"My mother claimed I'd be the death of her," Trevor went on. "Every new item she brought into the house was taken apart and put back together. I once ramped up and *improved* her new food processor so badly it turned everything she put in it into powder. In two seconds."

Jacey laughed. It felt good to laugh with him. It was nice that he indulged her. In all the time she'd known him and Caitlyn as a couple, he had rarely talked about himself.

"My mother was unimpressed with my suggestion that powder could be *useful*. I was unable to reverse the changes so, to my delight, I inherited the food processor and experimented with pulverizing everything from wood blocks to my cousin's fashion doll."

She laughed again, not unaware of how nice it was to laugh while the storm raged outside the cozy capsule they were in. "I think you were the rotten kid in that movie about toys, weren't you?"

"I only did that to one toy. It was after she ratted me out for letting the cat in my room. She was over visiting, and she kept chasing that poor cat, who despised her, as cats are known to do to people who want to force themselves upon them."

"The cat wasn't allowed in your room? Because of the food processor on steroids?"

"Nah, I had allergies. See? I told you I was a nerd more than a junior mad scientist. Anyway, my mother proved to be a bit of an investigator herself, because she sifted through that powder and determined doll demise.

"I had to save money from mowing lawns for a long time to replace both the doll and the food processor. Well worth it on the road to scientific investigation, though!"

Jacey was delighted at this unexpected insight into him, and his laughter joined hers.

Far from glazing over, Jacey found herself enjoying this. She liked the way his face looked as he remembered family memories. She had met his mom and dad at his and Caitlyn's wedding, and again at their housewarming.

His mom in particular had been in and out of the house a lot, in those horrible days of Caitlyn's illness.

Trevor came from the solid, good old-fashioned stuff families were made of.

Even though she wouldn't say she *knew* them, Trevor's folks were working-class people just bursting with pride at their son's accomplishments and joy at his happiness.

In sharp contrast, of course, to her own father. Jacey felt an almost greedy enjoyment of glimpses into Trevor. She could picture him mowing lawns, and she could picture him with those dark curls awry, his tongue caught between his teeth, taking apart his mother's prized possessions, his glee at avenging himself with his cousin's doll.

"So how does one go from taking apart Mom's food blender and pulverizing the annoying relative's toys to the heady world of the rich and famous?" she asked him, lightly.

"I'd love to tell you my path to good fortune was created by my skill, smarts and savvy, but no. It was blind luck. Like winning a lottery.

"I was called into a plant to troubleshoot a machine they constantly had trouble with. I redesigned a part for it. That single part revolutionized the way that machine operated. And there are millions of those machines around the world.

"I get a royalty every time one of my parts is sold. I'm always astonished when some engineering or business firm wants me to speak at their conference, or some magazine wants me on the cover."

Jacey found his humility endearing.

"Besides, being rich and famous didn't do me one iota of good when I set my sights on Caitlyn," he remembered. "After I came clean that I wasn't really a ski bum, I tried to apologize with an emerald bracelet. The expense suggested it came directly from the tomb of Cleopatra. She handed it back to me and told me that was way too easy. She expected time and energy and creativity be put into winning her, not money. Or baubles. That's what she called that bracelet. A bauble."

The air between them was suddenly saturated with that same feeling as when he had told her about his reaction to Caitlyn's choice of the pink chairs.

Love, the most dangerous thing of all, was in the air between them. They both let the silence go for a while and then he changed the subject.

"Tell me about this fear of flying," he said. "Amazing that you got on a plane to come. In fact, you came every time she asked. The wedding. The housewarming."

He didn't mention the last time Jacey had come.

"Oh, you know," she said. "They make drugs for that."

He laughed, as she had hoped he would. It occurred to her his laughter could very easily become an addiction, something a person wanted more and more and more of.

"Besides, it makes you a better person, facing fear. Even traversing icy roads that lead deep into the unknown could be seen as part of what makes life worth living."

"You know airplanes are safe, right?"

"Of course! You just told me. Safer than my bathroom."

"Well, statistically—"

"Never mind statistics!"

He raised an eyebrow at her. It was very Sean Connery being sexily surprised and amused. "You're talking to an engineer. Statistics are my life."

She lifted a shoulder.

He laughed again. She loved the sound, deep and rich, oblivious to the dangers that swirled around them outside this vehicle.

"Statistics only tell part of the story," she told him. "You can never know everything. Like, what if the pilot is hungover?"

"Airlines have very strict bottle to throttle rules."

"They do?"

"Yeah, a pilot can't fly within eight hours of

having a drink. Many airlines have a twelve-hour rule."

"Okay, what if it's something more subtle? A fight with a friend? A sick child? A messy divorce?"

"Has anybody ever told you, you worry too much?"

"Oh. Constantly." It had been a flaw even before Caitlyn's death, before the end of her relationship, before Johnny's colossal failure. "My catastrophe radar is constantly up and searching."

He glanced pointedly at the coffee in her hand. "You seem pretty relaxed right now. Is that laced with something?"

"Ha-ha, you ordered it from the drive-through window. If it's laced with something, that's on you. I'm not much of a drinker, anyway."

He nodded. "I can tell."

What did that mean? That she looked like a stick-in-the-mud? Didn't know how to let loose?

"If you were any kind of a drinker," he said, "I'm sure you would have turned to it a long time before now." His approval was subtle, but there nonetheless.

Oh! That was better than being thought a stick-in-the-mud: that she had handled the pressure of a friend dying without crutches.

How aware she was that it would be entirely too easy to follow her life pattern and twist herself into a pretzel for the prize of Trevor's approval.

"Besides," he said, sensing they were going somewhere maybe they didn't want to go, "I'd hate to arrive in Banff with a sloppy drunk music teacher under my care."

Despite the terrible conditions outside, there was something so soothing about the way Trevor handled the vehicle, the warmth and the music. Yesterday's traveling, the strain of the storm, a life unexpectedly fraught with emotion and surprises, caught up with her.

Jacey's head felt heavy. Her eyes closed. Twice, she managed to jerk herself awake, aware of the irony. She, who sniffed out the potential for catastrophe, who vibrated with apprehensive tension for what could go wrong next, was totally relaxed.

In the middle of a snowstorm. No, a squall. More dangerous than a blizzard.

Her head nodded again. She surrendered to the sensations.

Of being safe. Of being looked after.

CHAPTER SIX

JACEY WAS NOT sure how long she slept, but the slowing of the vehicle woke her up. In sleep her head had fallen sideways over the center console, until it was resting against his arm. She was appalled to find she had drooled on Trevor's sleeve!

"Where are we?" she asked, snapping her spine straight, blinking, disoriented.

She looked out the window. The snow was still falling extremely heavily. On either side of the vehicle were thick, shadowed stands of enormous evergreens.

Out the front windshield, through the veil of snow, she could see a series of adorable little rock cottages, with pitched roofs and Tudor-style slats on the steep gable ends.

"We're at the entrance to Banff National Park. These are the gatehouses."

Was she really awake?

"This looks like something out of a fairy tale," she said, awed. "It's like we're entering a magical kingdom."

He looked over at her.

"And indeed we are," he said, quietly.

Fairy tales, Trevor reminded himself, had happy endings, something he had lost faith in. Really, Jacey should have, too. Still, he could not harden himself to her wonder, or to his admiration that that quality had survived in her after the challenges of the past couple of years.

They stopped in the parking area just beyond the gatehouses after he had purchased his pass for the park.

She tumbled from the vehicle, her phone out, taking pictures of the gatehouses, tilting back her head to catch snow on her tongue, laughing. She put away her phone and picked up some snow. She made an inexpert snowball and tossed it at him. He dodged easily out of the way.

"You remind me of a puppy who has never seen snow before," he told her, but indulgently.

"Of course, we have snow in Toronto. But not like this! It's so…pristine. Even the air is different. Pure." She took a deep breath.

The mountains were, of course, gorgeous, but the conditions could also be deadly to the naive. Her mittens, the woolen kind, were still packed in her suitcase and she hadn't bothered to retrieve them before getting out of the vehicle.

Trevor felt a surge of responsibility for her.

No, it was more than responsibility. Protective-ness. He contemplated that uneasily.

"Come on," he said, "get back in the vehicle. That jacket isn't right for this weather. And you're going to freeze your hands."

Reluctantly, she obeyed, blowing on her fin-gertips.

In another half hour, they were on the main street of the world famous Township of Banff.

As it was known to do in these mountains, the weather shifted. The snow lightened and swirled and just as they exited the vehicle the clouds thinned to reveal the craggy magnificence of Cascade Mountain, which towered over Banff Avenue.

Even for him, cynic that he proclaimed himself to be, Trevor could see the early-morning light making an effort to pierce the clouds. Crystals of ice in the air looked like glitter. It was, indeed, like something out of a fairy tale.

But then the cloud thickened again, and the storm resumed unabated. The wind howled down off Cascade, and then the clouds enveloped it, making it invisible.

"Oh," Jacey said, taking it all in and hugging herself against the wind in her inadequate jacket. "It's amazing. The quintessential mountain vil-lage. Look at all the people."

It was true. The streets of the village were

clogged with people in colorful parkas and various hats.

"You can feel it in the air," Jacey said, that wonder still strong in her.

He could definitely feel something in the air; he just wasn't sure what it was. Until she clarified.

"Happiness," she said, cocking her head as if she could *hear* it as well as see it. And you could hear it: in laughter; in breathless conversations; in the odd exuberant shout.

After all his time in darkness, it felt jarring and vaguely dangerous. As if he might catch it.

"Of course they're happy," he said gruffly. "It's snowing and they're skiers and boarders anticipating fresh powder on the slopes. Let's go get you some, er, mittens. I'm sure you can tell from making your one snowball that the mittens you brought aren't going to cut it."

"I'm afraid you're probably right. And I might take a break from the fireplace to win a snowball fight with you!"

He held open the door of a ski shop he was familiar with.

She stepped in, then looked around, wide-eyed. The shop had a woodsy cabin feel to it, including a fire in a hearth at one end, crossed snowshoes, antique skis and animal mounts hanging from walls that looked like weathered logs.

"Look! There they are!" She went over to a bin,

overflowing with mittens, not unlike the ones she already had. Cute, but not particularly practical.

"Let's have a look at these gloves instead," he suggested, guiding her to a rack.

She joined him at the rack. She flipped over a pair of gloves and squinted at the price tag.

"It looks very expensive in here," she said nervously.

"In skiing, you kind of get what you pay for."

"But I'm not skiing," she reminded him. "I might throw a few snowballs. I'm not paying over a hundred dollars to throw snowballs, no matter how warm it keeps my hands. I'll suffer instead!"

He took a deep breath.

"That was Caitlyn's point, I think," he said, softly. "You've suffered enough."

Her mouth worked. She looked as if she might cry. Which, while terrible, he had to look at pragmatically.

She was sensitive right now. It was a good time to hit her with the truth.

"Caitlyn wanted you to go skiing. There are lift passes for both of us. And there's a lesson voucher for you."

"I don't have any of the stuff to go skiing," she said. "I don't even have skis."

"Well, skis are easy. We can rent those. The rest of this stuff we'll have to buy." He fished in his pocket and handed her a list.

She turned her attention to it, and her lips moved

as she read: ski pants, jacket, gloves, goggles, toque, neck gator, long underwear, good socks.

The joy she had had at the gates and surveying the main street disappeared. He could see she was trying not to panic.

"You knew I needed all this. You've made a list."

"Yes."

"Why did you wait until now to tell me?"

"Is it a big deal?"

"Yes!"

"Survival in the elements is not an easy thing."

"I didn't think this all the way through," she said. "I can't—"

She clamped her mouth shut, but he could see the turmoil in her face. She might as well have finished the sentence. *She couldn't afford it.*

"I'm buying," he said.

She headed for the door. "No. I can't. Oh, why did I come? I knew this was a dumb idea. What was I—"

"Now?" he asked, incredulously. He cut her off, maneuvering around her, blocking the door.

"Let me by."

"Now, after you've traveled three thousand miles and convinced me to go along with this? *Now* you decided to have second thoughts?"

"Actually," she said stubbornly, "I was having second thoughts as soon as you mentioned the gondola. But I'll do that. I'll do all the parts we don't need *lists* for. How's that sound?"

"Like I'm negotiating with a terrorist," he said dryly.

"We can go to the resort, without the skiing for me. That's the expensive part, right? Really, Trevor, I'm *happy* with a book."

In her comfort zone. Not taking any chances. Except for the gondola part, which was hardly a concession.

"Look," he said patiently, "the ski lift vouchers were in that package Caitlyn put together. It included a lesson for you. That's the expensive part. And it's all already been paid for. What do you want to do with those?"

He'd hit the right button. The pragmatic part of her didn't want to see all that money wasted. He pressed his advantage.

"It *was* Caitlyn's wish. You honored her by delivering it. You got me to go along when I didn't really want to. Jacey, we've come this far."

She looked flustered. She went over to a rack of jackets and turned over a sleeve of one, looking at the price tag. She went very pale.

"I can't accept this kind of gift. And I certainly can't afford it."

"Well, you can't go skiing in the jacket you have on."

She frowned. "I should have gone to the secondhand store before I came." Then she brightened. "We could find a secondhand store."

"We're not finding a secondhand store!"

"Snob."

"No, I'm being practical. I don't know where one is. And we don't know if they would have what you need in your size."

She contemplated that dubiously.

He took a deep breath. "Jacey, you lost your house and your marriage over us. This is the least I can do."

Her chin tilted up proudly. "I would never accept payment for what I did for you. Never. It wasn't really for you. At least, not just for you. Being there for Caitlyn was for me, too!"

"What is it with people like you?"

"People like me?"

"Yes, people like you," Trevor said, his voice patient but with a deliberately stern note inserted. "You can give endlessly but you can't ever accept anything back. Did you ever consider the fact that other people like to give, too? That it's as much a blessing to accept a gift as to give one?"

"No," she said stubbornly.

"Let someone do something for you," he said. "Let *me* do something for you."

"You don't *owe* me anything just because I came to be with you when my best friend needed me. You're insulting me."

"Maybe you're insulting me," he snapped back. It occurred to him they were having an argument.

And that he wasn't winning it. She was still trying to slide around him, tiny step by tiny step, toward the door. What was she going to do when she got there? Go sit in the vehicle with her nose in the air until he found a secondhand store?

"For God's sake," he said to her, hoping their bickering wasn't entertaining some bored sales-clerk hiding behind a rack of jackets, "Let me be nice."

"You already are nice!"

"A minute ago you told me I was a snob."

"Well, besides that—and the pulverizing of your cousin's doll—you seem pretty nice."

"No, I'm not!" he said.

"Caitlyn wouldn't have married you if you weren't!" she crowed as if the argument was won.

The argument. Geez. He was standing in a very public, very expensive, store, arguing.

It felt oddly invigorating.

"Let's get something straight," he told her. "Guys aren't nice. It doesn't come naturally to us. We're self-centered, self-indulgent narcissists for the most part. Don't you see? Caitlyn would have approved of this. Of me being generous and helpful. She was on a mission to make me a bet-ter man."

Jacey stopped moving toward the door.

"No," she said, firmly, those green eyes sparking. "She wasn't. She gave you the best gift of all, you numbskull. She loved you exactly as you were."

"Did you just call me a numbskull?" he asked, incredulous.

They stared at each other.

The tension broke when she giggled. He found himself smiling. Thankfully, that friction that had risen between them dissipated as quickly and as furiously as that storm.

"Yes, I did. I'm sorry."

"You don't sound very sincere."

"Because what kind of numbskull would think Caitlyn was trying to remake you into something you weren't?"

"You just called me that again. Okay, maybe she wasn't *trying* to remake me. But I became better, because of her, whether that was her intention or not."

Jacey's mouth worked. She wanted to argue, he could tell. He didn't remember her being this aggravating.

"So," he said, feeling like Beast wanting Belle to have dinner with him, "allow me to make kindness part of Caitlyn's legacy."

He was aware he was practically begging her to let him be nice to her.

Jacey's face softened. Her green eyes swelled up with tenderness. That look felt as if it would slay the very part of him he had guarded so tenaciously since the death of his wife.

"Okay," she agreed.

"There's one other thing. No, two."

"What?" There was that querulous tone of voice again, as if she was already giving up way too much by allowing him to buy her anything, and now he was daring to ask for more. "Now who sounds like a terrorist negotiating?"

"You can't look at any of the price tags."

"Of course I'm looking at price tags. Are you crazy?"

"Apparently," he said dryly. "A crazy numbskull."

"What's the other condition?"

"You have to have fun. Like a kid in a candy store."

She looked mutinous.

"Caitlyn's wish," he reminded her. "Have fun."

"I think I could grow to hate you, Trevor Cooper."

"For asking you to have fun?"

"For backing me up against a wall by using Caitlyn's wish. I'll accept your offer to outfit me for the slopes. But reluctantly. The other two things—not looking at price tags and having fun—I have to think about. Spending money is not fun for me. Even someone else's."

He sighed. "What is it with me and women who hate my money?"

"It's a curse," she agreed, but there was a small, rewarding smile playing across her lips as she turned back to that very expensive rack of parkas.

CHAPTER SEVEN

JACEY FINGERED THE jacket and contemplated the task she'd been given. Have fun. Spending someone else's money. Trevor's money, specifically.

Why not? Why was it so hard for her to accept good things?

Well, where was the line between accepting good things and being seen as a charity case?

She moved on from the jacket she knew to be very expensive. It was very difficult not to look around for a sales rack. Places like this probably didn't even have sales racks, particularly since they were in the height of the winter season.

She pulled out a solid battleship-gray jacket that looked puffy and warm, if unexciting. She held it up to Trevor.

"No," Trevor said, with barely a glance at it.

"Why? What's wrong with it? It looks very serviceable."

He came and took the jacket from her hand, hanging it firmly back on the rack. It was quite an arrogant thing to do, really.

Why did something sigh inside her at the prospect of someone just making the decisions for her? Someone who was clearly intent on spoiling her?

"I'm guessing you're a size small, right?"

Don't let this man railroad your life. On the other hand, it *would* be interesting to see what he chose for her.

He pushed through the jackets, paused, pulled one from the rack and held it out. It was a collage of possibly the brightest colors Jacey had ever seen.

That was how he saw her?

"It looks very wild." She squeaked a halfhearted protest. Everything in her leaned toward it. The jacket, with its unexpected flamboyant colors, was extraordinary. Mostly white, it looked as if paint—in iridescent peacock-emerald greens and stunning blues—had been splotched on it randomly. Only a very bold person could wear that.

It wasn't her, at all. It was for someone who loved life. Who embraced it. Who knew how to have fun. Did he really see her like that?

"That would be a good jacket for someone who is an expert skier, who *wants* people to look at them."

"That's quite a lot to read into a jacket," he said. "So what if it makes people look at you?"

Oh! To have that kind of confidence!

"You'll look perfectly adorable practicing your snowplow."

Perfectly adorable. Is that how she wanted Trevor to see her? As perfectly adorable, like a golden retriever puppy? Of course that was how she wanted him to see her!

As a trusted friend, she told herself firmly. Though what woman wouldn't want such a handsome man to see her as an attractive, *sexy* trusted friend?

"They aren't my colors," she said, firmly.

"Really? Tell your suitcase."

Though she'd told him it was a strategic purchase to help her find it easily amongst the other passengers' luggage, that wasn't the whole truth. The suitcase had appealed to her for the very same reason her couch did. It somehow expressed a lightheartedness she longed for.

"This jacket choice is the very same thing!" Trevor insisted.

"I'm not seeing the connection."

"I won't be able to lose you on the slopes any more than you'd be able to lose that luggage at the baggage claim."

Jacey felt dashed at the reason for his choice. It wasn't because he saw her as having the potential to be bold and fun—albeit adorable—instead of timid and retiring. It was practical!

But trepidation squeezed out her disappointment as she registered his reasons for choosing that jacket.

"You can lose someone on the slopes?" she asked, trying to keep her tone casual.

"Sure." He was still sorting through outerwear, now holding up a pair of brightly colored ski slacks that matched the jacket and squinting at them appraisingly.

"Like how lost?" Jacey pressed. "Out of view for a few minutes?"

"It's happened. Skiers get separated. You saw what the weather is like out there. What do you think of these?" He held up the pants for her inspection.

If they reduced her chances of getting lost, she liked them very much! She snatched them from his hands.

"What about *really* lost?" she asked him. "Like wandering through the freezing wilderness *lost*? I've seen that."

"In Toronto?" he asked, raising an amused eyebrow at her.

"On the news!"

"I'm not going to let you be the topic of a news story, Jacey."

"There are things outside of your control, you know."

"Yeah," he said, a hint of bitterness in his voice, "I know."

This, Jacey told herself, was not why Caitlyn

had sent her on this mission. It wasn't to remind him things were out of his control, but to coax him, a wounded bear, out of his cave, back into the sunlight.

"Bears!" she said. "Have you ever seen a bear while skiing?"

The change of topic, as absurd as it was, did exactly what she had hoped. The bitterness melted from him as the lovely lines of his mouth quirked upward.

But her enjoyment was short-lived at his answer.

"I have," he said solemnly.

So seeing a bear was not absurd? "Do I need bear spray?"

"They don't like bright colors," he said.

"You're teasing me."

"I am," he agreed.

The thing was she kind of enjoyed being teased by him.

"Though I have, indeed, seen bears while skiing. Just not at this time of year. You'll sometimes see them in the spring."

Note to self: *never* ski in the spring. A possibility so remote, she didn't even have to make a note to herself.

He looked at his watch. "We better make some time if we're going to get in a few runs today. Come on, let's wrap this up."

Together, they chose toques and socks and

gloves until she was staggering under the weight of them as she made her way to the change room.

It was only once she was there, her bounty laid out before her like pirate's treasure, that she realized she had had fun.

Just like a kid in a candy store.

"When you find anything you like that fits," he called through the closed door, "just leave it on. Next stop, Moonbeam."

When she emerged from the change room, he grinned at her.

"You look awesome," he said. "As if you've been skiing your whole life. As if you're ready to win your gold medal."

He stepped in very close to her.

For a moment her heart stopped.

Why on earth would she think the warmth in his eyes and the easiness of his smile was going to translate to a kiss?

If he tried to kiss her, she told herself firmly, she wouldn't kiss back. He was Caitlyn's husband!

In fact, she would *hate* him if he tried to kiss her. She might have to slap him. Good grief! They were friends. She couldn't respect him— or herself—if that boundary was crossed!

As it turned out, Jacey's brief and silent debate was akin to debating whether the most dangerous thing was a bathroom or love—pointless. Because Trevor wasn't moving in to kiss her.

He wasn't even moving in to tuck a stray strand of hair under her toque, which, oddly, would have been almost as alarming as being kissed by him.

No, he moved close and with lightning swiftness found each price tag from each item and snapped them off.

"You can wait outside while I pay."

Really? She should have protested. But it was nice that he wanted to protect her from the shock of the expense of it all and she was so unsettled by her kiss thoughts, she couldn't speak.

When she emerged from the store in her new, splashy, outdoor wear, Jacey discovered an amazing metamorphosis had occurred.

It was still snowing, and hard. But even that felt different. Not threatening. Because she was one of them now, part of this colorful throng, celebrating the snow. As she looked around, she realized she looked *exactly* like all the people on the streets, in their bright jackets and snazzy toques.

But what was more, she felt like them, too.

Happy.

Ready for the next stop. Moonbeam Peaks.

Not just Moonbeam, but three days and two nights at Moonbeam with him. The guy who was, if she was being honest, probably the true source of her happiness.

Except it turned out to be not exactly true, that their next stop was Moonbeam.

Their next stop was the gondola, which was

the only route to Moonbeam. An enclosed go-cart arrived at their vehicle when they parked in the spot reserved for hotel guests. All their luggage was loaded and they were chauffeured to a little station at the foot of an absolutely gigantic mountain.

Even the storm could not hide how humungous it was. And rocky. And high.

And moving up it, like ants in a determined line, were steel cages swinging from a cable, that while thick, did not appear to Jacey's amateur eye to be up to the task of holding all that weight.

"How many gondolas do you think there are?" she asked Trevor, subdued.

"I think this gondola is one of the largest in the world at seven kilometers. I'd guess there are maybe a hundred and fifty cars."

"That's a lot of weight."

He reached out and gave her gloved hand a squeeze. "They're still accident-free, after all these years of operation. Imagine that."

Of course, what Jacey imagined was they were about due.

"It seems to go very high," she said. She started reading the "fun fact" sign beside the line they were in but none of the facts seemed particularly fun to her.

Every single item that went to or left Moonbeam was delivered by this apparatus. More weight! They would be two hundred feet off the ground when the car they were in reached its highest point! It traveled at nearly 20 feet a second, which meant they were going to be trapped on it for more than twenty minutes!

Jacey felt her stomach dip. And then that awful, familiar feeling of her palms sweating. She slid off one glove, and then the other, wiping her palms on her new pant leg.

As they edged closer to their turn to get on, the happiness dried up in Jacey as if she'd been turned from a grape to a raisin in the span of three seconds.

She watched as one of the cars loaded, those brightly dressed, happy people disappearing inside it.

Within seconds, as if it had been shot from a catapult, the gondola was up in the air—way up in the air—dangling from that grotesquely thin arm and disappearing into the storm.

Sweat beaded on her brow. Her stomach swirled a little more vigorously.

And then she was that little girl in the concert hall. Just like now, she had been all dressed up then, ready for her big moment, though that night she'd been in the pretty dress that she and her father had chosen together.

She remembered being led out to the grand piano, all those people watching her, her father beaming with pride as he adjusted the bench for her, opened the music book and placed it in front of her.

Just like now, it had felt momentous, like some kind of turning point, like her life would never be the same.

And therein lay the problem, then as now.

Jacey liked things to stay the same.

Trevor returned the gondola attendant's smile as he waved them forward. Their luggage was loaded on, along with Trevor's skis.

When Jacey didn't move, Trevor nudged her. She still didn't move.

He glanced down at her and noticed her face was very pale. Was there a little bead of sweat over her upper lip?

"I can't," she whispered.

For a horrible moment he thought she might faint. He tugged her out of the line and nodded at the attendant to let the gondola—with their luggage on it—go. The next group gave them a curious look, then shuffled by them.

Trevor took her by the arm and guided her out of the line and around the corner of the gondola station.

The wind whipped at them.

"What's up?" he said, carefully casual.

"I told you. I'm afraid of heights. I thought I could get over it, but I can't. Trevor, did you see how skinny that arm is that's holding the car onto the cable?"

"Yes," he said agreeably, "it's an engineering marvel."

She gave him a baleful look. "It can't possibly be safe."

He knew he could reiterate to her how safe the gondola was. He knew he could check his phone for all the facts in the world and present them to her.

And he knew that it wouldn't help. Not one little bit.

CHAPTER EIGHT

"So that's why we're really here," Trevor said to Jacey. He congratulated himself on the unfamiliar gentle tone in his voice. He was doing it! He was being a better man.

That better man knew exactly what to do next. He pulled her deep into his arms and held her so tight he could feel her heart beating, even through the thick padding of both their ski jackets. Her heart was going way too fast, as if she was a rabbit running from frothing-at-the-mouth dogs.

"What do you mean?" her muffled voice asked him.

"My beautiful, sensitive, intuitive wife knew it wasn't about being you—us—being happy. She set this up on the pretext of having fun, but that's not really what it's about."

"Yes," Jacey said, peeking around him to gaze balefully at the gondola cars going up the wire, "because anyone can see that *thing* is not fun."

"It's about not being scared anymore," he told her. "Terrified that life is just waiting to deliver some new dastardly blow, some horrible surprise."

"Like a gondola falling off a cable," Jacey agreed. She sighed her relief that he *got* it.

"That's why she arranged all of this, Jacey. Caitlyn knew we can't be happy until we get over the fear that's holding us back."

Jacey pulled her head out of his jacket and scanned his face.

"You're not afraid," she said.

"Yeah, I am," he said softly, amazed to be admitting this thing he had never admitted, not even to himself. "Of everything. Since the day she died."

"I was afraid way before that. It just confirmed—"

"I know," he said softly.

"You do?"

And he felt as if he did know her. Completely. Her every fear and her every insecurity. As well as his own. It made him feel the most frightening tenderness for her.

"This is what happens when you least expect it," he told her, though really he was thinking out loud.

Yes, this is what happened when you forgot to protect yourself. When you said yes instead of no.

He wasn't sure he was ready for this, but it already felt as if it was way too late to try and go back now.

"Life's asking more of us," he said. "Do you hear it? Listen."

She cocked her head and they heard the whir and clunk of the machinery, the cars on the cables, and beyond that, the storm howling down the mountain.

"Life is asking us to be stronger than we were before. And braver than we've ever been. I can't do it without you." Trevor was absolutely stunned by how true this was. He was aware, even though they had not had much contact over the past two years, that he treasured her friendship.

Her eyes were locked on his, searching. She found whatever it was she was looking for.

"Okay," she said, her voice trembling, "I'm ready now."

"Are you sure?"

She nodded and left the protection of his chest. Her hand reached for his, though. He took it, but it wasn't good enough for her.

She took off that brand-new glove, and he knew instantly what she wanted. A touch that would be skin to skin, warmth to warmth, person to person. He took his glove off, too.

When her hand came to be in his, he could feel her heartbeat in the pulse that ran between her thumb and her pointer finger. Her heart was still racing. He could also feel the whole world shift. He had held her hand last night and it hadn't felt like this.

What was changing?

The truth?

Everything.

He was coming back to life, whether he wanted to or not.

The gondolas were designed for four people, or two who had luggage. Since their luggage had gone without them, Trevor and Jacey really should have been put on a gondola with another party of two. But the attendant took one look at them when they came back around the corner of the station and held up his hand to the people who were supposed to get on next.

He gestured Trevor and Jacey forward and they ducked into the gondola and took the seats facing up the mountain, side by side.

The attendant shut the door behind them.

"I think that's what a prison door sounds like when it shuts," she said.

"You can't know that."

"Ha. Movies."

"Well, this is twenty minutes, not twenty to life."

He was rewarded with a stifled giggle, but then Trevor felt every single fiber of Jacey tense as the gondola car trundled forward, the bar caught the cable and they soared.

He moved close to her. He put his hand around her shoulder, and tugged her yet closer, feeling the deep connection of shared experience between them.

All through those days of Caitlyn dying, Jacey had been there for him. Now it was his turn.

"Breathe," he whispered to her.

She seemed to contemplate that.

"Try Ujjayi," he teased gently.

She was silent, and then she said, "Prepare for a karate chop to the throat."

He laughed, and then she laughed, just a little bit. He felt some of the tension drain from her rigid shoulders.

"This is the similarity to prison. We can't get out if we change our minds," she noted.

"Well, technically, you probably could."

"I think we're locked in."

He reached over her, as if he was going to try the door lever and test her theory. She squealed her protest.

"No! Don't touch it."

"We could be the first accident on the gondola," he said. "Death by exit at two hundred feet."

She closed her eyes. "I don't think we're at two hundred feet yet. Don't tease me. It's not funny."

He liked teasing her, and he suspected she liked it, too, because she snuggled closer to him, and he tightened his grip on her shoulders. Her new toque, fuzzy, tickled his nose.

"I can't believe you got me on it!" She tilted

her head and leveled him a look. He saw the deep green of her eyes taking him in, taking him *all* in.

It was unsettling to feel this *known*.

Of course, she did know him. And she'd known him long before now. She had seen him every single day of the battle he had ultimately lost.

It was not news to her that he was afraid. He just wondered why she had gotten on the gondola with him instead of running the other way.

Every word he had spoken to her had been his deepest truth. He felt stripped bare by it.

She leaned back in the chair, closed her eyes, to avoid looking out the window, he suspected.

"My mom died when I was eight," she told him in a low voice.

"Caitlyn told me you were raised by a single dad."

"It was me and my dad against the world. He was a musician, and music provided us both solace. After my mom died, I really lost myself in it. Nothing brought me comfort like sitting at the piano, not just playing music, but becoming music.

"My dad felt I was gifted. I had the best teachers and even they thought I was extraordinarily talented. I think my father found solace from his own pain in my immersion in this new world. I think it allowed him to feel successful as a father when most days he just felt bewildered and in way over his head. My piano became his focus and my escape.

"When I was twelve, my teacher arranged for me to do a solo concert. It was an incredible honor to be asked. The who's-who of the music world were going to be there.

"But I got out in front of the audience, and I froze.

"I could not do it. I could not persuade myself. My father could not persuade me. I was absolutely paralyzed.

"I had the same feeling looking at the gondolas, just now. When I lost my mom, the world changed irrevocably for me. I've hated change ever since then. And some part of me, even though I felt frozen, powerless, like I wanted to play more than anything in the world, knew if I did, things would change again in ways I could not control."

"I'm not sure getting in the gondola has the power to change your life in quite the same way."

"But it does. You said it. It's about facing fear to live fully."

"Where's your father now?" he asked.

"He died of cancer five years ago." Jacey hesitated. "I wish we could have fixed things between us before he died."

"In what way?"

"I don't ever think he got over the sense of being betrayed by me that day."

"That's not reasonable. You said you were twelve!"

"He lost interest in my musical development after that. It was the interest we shared, the thing that glued us together. But no matter where I went musically after that, he would always see it through the lens of my best opportunity having been thrown away."

"I'm sorry," Trevor said. "I'm sorry you didn't have a chance to repair things between you."

"Why couldn't he understand? If I could have done it for him, I would have. You know, I've never, ever played publicly since that day? Not even once. I love teaching. I love playing. But I can't perform. I think it's probably exposed my deepest fears—making a mistake, losing control, being embarrassed."

Jacey considered what she had just revealed to Trevor. There it was: the root fear at the heart of all her other fears. And she had trusted him with it.

When he was silent for a long, long time she thought she had revealed too much of herself. Allowed herself, because she felt so vulnerable, to share more deeply and more personally than their relationship warranted.

"What if," he said finally, slowly, "it wasn't about fear of change at all that night at the concert hall? What if it wasn't any of those things?

Fear of making a mistake, or loss of control or being embarrassed?"

Something in her went very still.

She opened her eyes and looked at him, puzzled, and yet she could feel some hope fluttering to life within her, too.

He seemed to be able to see something she had never seen.

"What if," Trevor continued quietly, "you didn't want to share that space, that sacred place that gave you such solace from the pain of losing your mom? What if you didn't want to share that with the world? What if it was yours and yours alone?"

Her mouth fell open. Tears filled her eyes. "I've never once thought of it in any other way except as my greatest failure."

"What if you look at it as if taking tremendous courage to keep your gift to yourself instead of giving it away?"

The tears fell.

"Look," he said. "Look out the window."

Jacey did not want to look out the window. She wanted to pretend the whole world was the three feet they shared, the feeling she had with his arm around her, and her head nestled into his chest.

Of complete trust.

"Look," he said again. "Jacey, don't miss this."

The thing was she could feel the courage inside herself, like a small green stem, coming out of dirt, breaking through the crust of winter.

She turned her head ever so slightly. Through the blur of her tears, she saw shafts of light were beginning to pierce the snowstorm. Weak at first, and then stronger and stronger, until they burst out above the cloud entirely, and a whole brilliant world of rugged rock, untouched snow, shadowed forests and endless blue skies was revealed to them.

Jacey felt overwhelmed by the beauty.

"You see?" he said, that gorgeous deep voice so gentle. He touched her face, wiped the tears away, one by one.

"Yes," she said. "I see. I've made some kind of breakthrough, and the whole world is a reflection of that."

"I meant do you see we're nearly halfway there and the cable is holding?"

What's the worst danger in the world? Bathrooms? Or love?

They were fated to see the world so differently. Or were they? She took her eyes off the amazing view for one second and looked at him. She wasn't the least bit fooled about what he really meant.

She wanted to run her hand over the line of his jaw, trace his nose with her fingertips, smooth down his rooster tail.

Instead, she tucked that errant hand inside her

pocket, ashamed of herself. She could know him deeply without complicating their relationship by touching him!

Still, she could not stop the next words from spilling from her lips. "I see why Caitlyn loved you."

"Because I'm extraordinarily handsome?"

She laughed.

But then he said, softly, ever so softly, "I see why she loved you, too."

CHAPTER NINE

JACEY COULD FEEL something within her lifting up, as if her spirit was reflecting the motion of the cable car as it went up and up and up. She and Trevor were in a place human beings rarely experienced.

Birds experienced this.

This place of suspension and motion, a dance between the earth and the sky.

People on airplanes might know this, but to a lesser extent. The flying experience did not have this immediacy. It did not have this silence that felt oddly and beautifully sacred.

Jacey thought this was likely exactly what Caitlyn had hoped when she had made this elaborate plan for her best friend and her husband.

That her love for both of them could heal what seemed beyond healing.

Of course, Jacey needed to fight the feeling that the exhilaration was in some way because of Trevor. It was *with* him, and that was a very important distinction. Conquering her fear had left her wide-open, and she would have to guard carefully that she was not so open that forbidden feelings for her best friend's husband crept in.

Jacey was actually sorry when the cable car journey ended. The gondola ride finished right at the center of the Village of Moonbeam. As Trevor helped her from the gondola, she looked around herself, trying to take it all in.

She had thought Banff was quaint and lovely, but Moonbeam Peaks was like a village constructed of gingerbread. Deep snow dripped from the steep roofs of log cottages. Rock-fronted shops and small boutique hotels lined a gently curving, snow-clogged main pathway. The sun was brilliant on all that snow, sparking and glittering with the flashing blue light of diamonds.

Ski racks were the hitching posts of the village. There were several in front of every building, all of them filled with skis and boards. The equipment was like artwork with its graphic, bright designs. Poles stood on their own, planted in the snow.

People in colorful jackets, goggles set up on their toques, walked awkwardly in huge boots, sometimes with skis on their shoulders.

Moonbeam Mountain soared behind the village, mighty and majestic. Its pristine slopes looked like mounds of perfect whipping cream and were dotted with skiers coming down them. And skiers and boarders going up, on chairlifts, their legs attached to their equipment, dangling into air beneath them.

Was she going to use a chairlift? It looked even more terrifying than the cable car! But somehow, shockingly, Jacey realized even though her stomach did a little dipsy-doodle at the thought of riding a chairlift, she wasn't quite sure if it was terror. Could she actually be *excited*?

She was aware of having been dropped into a *world* as foreign and as delightful as visiting a different country.

There were no motorized vehicles in this world, and it made all the other sounds—the humming of the chairlifts, people's voices blending together in many languages, laughter—seem amplified.

"I've never seen anything like this," she said to Trevor. "It's a place unto itself. It exists only to bring joy."

He laughed. "And maybe make some money."

She smacked his arm. "Stop it. You're not nearly as cynical as you want me to believe you are."

An open-aired golf cart whirred up, and she saw their luggage was already on board.

"Do you belong to this luggage? I'm Ozzie. I'm going to deliver you to your accommodations. And then—" he checked a notecard— "Jacey is scheduled for a ski lesson. So if it's okay with you, we'll just drop off your stuff and get you checked in, and then I'll take you to the Snow School."

They hopped on the backseat of the cart, Ozzie in the front. His long, dark hair hung out from under his Moonbeam Mountain staff toque. Except for the historical-romance-novel hair, he reminded Jacey of one of those firemen on the calendars.

"Honeymooners?" he asked them over his broad shoulder.

Jacey shot Trevor a look. An irritating awareness of him shivered along her spine and she sternly crushed it. Was there something between them after that connection that they had made on the cable car that would make Ozzie ask that?

Trevor looked annoyed. "Just friends," he said in a voice that didn't brook further conversation.

Yes, Jacey told herself firmly. Friends.

Ozzie dropped them at the door of Moonbeam Mountain Manor and said he would keep Trevor's skis on the cart and meet them at their room with the rest of their luggage.

The hotel lobby was lodge-like and gorgeous. The walls were constructed of logs, darkened to rich gold with age, and soaring twenty feet up to a timber-vaulted ceiling. A huge stone fireplace was at one end, a fire crackling in it. A baby grand piano was beside it. Deep furniture formed a U-shape around the fireplace and the piano.

"Are you going to play that?" Trevor asked her, nodding at the piano.

"Oh, no," she said, uneasily. "It's kind of out in the open."

"I'd like to hear you, though."

"Someday," she told him insincerely. "I'm more interested in that armchair and the fireplace, though I think for now my plan of retreating to a safe and familiar world of a book and a hot chocolate has been thwarted."

"You're right about that."

And as much as she normally hated the unexpected, she kind of liked that feeling in her tummy of anticipation, not knowing exactly what would happen next.

Her and Trevor's accommodations were at the end of a very long, wide hall.

Ozzie awaited them with their luggage.

"This is our presidential suite," Ozzie said as Trevor swiped the pass on the door. "And presidents have actually stayed here. And a princess once, too." He gave her a look and smiled charmingly. "Maybe twice," he said.

Trevor shot him a look. She giggled. Was Ozzie *flirting* with her? Crazy, but still feeling wide-open from her experience on the gondola, she *loved* it.

"Believe me, I'm no princess. Just a music tutor."

"I love music. I play the guitar."

"Not surprisingly," Trevor muttered.

"I'm thinking of giving up being a music tutor."

There. She'd said it out loud. Maybe because of her embracing of this adventure it didn't feel nearly as scary as she thought it would.

"How come?" Ozzie asked. "It sounds like the perfect job."

"Oh, you know what they say. Change is as good as a rest."

Trevor made a noise in his throat that sounded a bit like a growl. She turned and looked at him. He was leveling a look at Ozzie that was anything but friendly.

She frowned. One thing she had never pictured him as was a snob. And yet, he obviously did not appreciate the conversation between her and Ozzie.

"Would you like me to put the luggage away?" Ozzie offered. "Which ones would you like in which bedroom?"

Two bedrooms! It really was a suite. Jacey realized that she and Trevor no doubt looked every bit as platonic as they were; two friends on a ski trip.

But Trevor narrowed his eyes at Ozzie. "You can just leave the luggage there."

"I'll wait outside for you," Ozzie said, wagging his eyebrows at her.

"For God's sake," Trevor said once he had closed the door. "He's quite smitten."

"He's not!"

"He was trying to figure out our sleeping arrangements."

"He only offered to put our luggage away," she said mildly. "I think that's his job."

"Yeah, that's what you'll think until you hear a tapping on your window in the middle of the night."

It was absurd—okay, and a little delightful— that Trevor would read so much into the casual encounter.

"Do you always have that effect on men?"

"Come on! You've known me longer than that." She was sure Caitlyn had filled him in all about her introverted friend, just in case he hadn't figured it out for himself.

"Princess," he said with a scowl. "It's so lame."

She studied him. Was Trevor jealous?

"I feel very protective of you," he said when he saw her look.

Of course he wasn't jealous! That rated right up there with mistakenly thinking he was going to kiss her in the ski shop.

They were friends.

Friends. Friends. Friends.

"I mean, obviously you can do better than a guitar-playing ski bum."

"It would take a ski bum to know a ski bum, I'm sure," she said sweetly.

"I never played the guitar!"

"Perhaps he's really a bazzillionaire?"

"He's not."

"Trevor, the ink is barely dry on my divorce papers. I'm not interested." Honestly, she did not know whether to be annoyed or amused by his protectiveness. Or something else altogether.

Not aware of him as a man. That was off-limits! But rising toward what he was doing, allowing herself to feel cared about. Looked after.

"Speaking of bazzillionaires," she said, changing the subject, "look at this place."

Like the lobby of the lodge, this suite's walls were soaring logs, golden with age, that ended in an open vaulted ceiling. The furniture was mountain-cabin appropriate, but in a very sophisticated take on that theme. It had its own fireplace, and double-glass-paned doors looked out on the mountain. She could see skiers swooshing by, and she went to the doors.

There was a private deck out there.

Off to one side was a hot tub.

Here was the thing: she could not get in a hot tub with Trevor. It would be one of those moments—like taking the stage at a concert hall or getting on a gondola—that had the potential to change life forever.

This was so good the way it was, wasn't it?

They were close, but without complications. He was protective of her. Like a big brother. But when she slid him a look, the thumping of her heart gave something away.

With the slightest push, the feelings she had toward him would not be brotherly, at all! That thought made her feel horribly weak and small. Hadn't she suffered quite enough loss at the hands of love?

Not that she didn't care about him. Of course she cared about him! And deeply, too, but in that nice, safe way that you cared about your best friend's husband.

Friends, she repeated, like a mantra. She turned quickly and grabbed her suitcase. She tried one of the doors off the common area of the suite.

It opened to a room with a huge log bed at the center, plush bedding in sharp contrast to the deliberate rustic vibe of the furniture. It, too, had French doors that opened onto the deck. That hot tub was right in front of those doors!

"Uh, I think this is the master suite. I'll just—"

"No, you take it," he said. He came and glanced over her shoulder. "Fit for a princess," he decided, just a hint of something in his tone.

Not jealousy, obviously.

Sarcasm.

What a relief!

What was wrong with him? Trevor asked himself a few minutes later as they got back in the cart. He gave Ozzie a warning look.

He realized he was inordinately annoyed that Jacey had told a complete stranger she was considering changing careers, and not once mentioned it to him.

Ozzie was, apparently, oblivious to warning looks.

"What lessons are you taking?" he asked her.

"Beginner. It's my very first time."

"A virgin!" Ozzie crowed.

Trevor had to fight an uncharacteristic desire to punch him, especially when Jacey giggled and blushed as if they were discussing a passage out of the Kama Sutra.

Ozzie, oblivious to the dark look Trevor was leveling at the back of his head, said, "I meant are you going to take a ski lesson or a board lesson?"

To Trevor it felt as if this was a discussion *he* should be having with her.

"I thought I'd take a ski lesson. I mean, Trevor skis, so he can give me tips once I'm let loose on the hill."

Thanks for remembering I'm here, Trevor thought darkly, *though it's likely very unwise to mention being let loose with this guy.*

She was naive and thought Ozzie was just being friendly. But Trevor knew all about *that* look in a guy's eyes. Frank male appreciation. That *worth a try* look.

Well, seeing her through Ozzie's eyes, she did look adorable in the new snowsuit. The pants were hugging her lithe form, and little spikes of her hair were sticking out from under the toque.

But there was something a little more troubling about her than adorable.

And then it occurred to him what it was.

Jacey Tremblay looked kind of sexy.

Plus, there had been something about her that he had noticed as soon as they'd gotten off the cable car.

Shimmering in the air.

It wasn't just that she'd conquered a fear, though she had; there was something more confident in the way she carried herself.

There was also something more open about her, a veneer of reserve gone.

She probably didn't even know.

But Ozzie did.

That veneer had likely gone a long way to protecting her in the past.

She was more vulnerable than she realized. Trevor realized he was going to have to really watch out for her.

He thought of the hot tub that he had glimpsed out on the deck through the main bedroom balcony door.

He felt something stirring in him. He was aghast. Jacey was super vulnerable, and he felt it was his sworn mission to protect her from making bad choices. He'd lay down his life to do that for her if he had to.

There would be no bad choices from his end of things. None. He was not ready—would possibly never be ready again—for where the wrong choice, one moment of weakness, with Jacey could go.

CHAPTER TEN

TREVOR, IN HIS role as Jacey's protector, was relieved to see the last of Ozzie. With a backward wave of his hand, the ski resort employee drove off after dropping them in front of the ski school chalet. Still, he tried to make himself memorable by giving the little cart so much power the front wheels raised off the ground, like a horse rearing.

"I think that little cowboy maneuver was meant to impress you," Trevor told Jacey.

"I doubt it."

"He was flirting with you all the way here."

Jacey regarded him with surprise. And then amusement. "I'm not sure how a detailed description of how the garbage leaves the resort on a special cable car, painted to look like an elephant and named Dumpo, could be interpreted that way."

"It was the *way* he said it."

The look in her eyes told him he was being ridiculous. He wasn't! Guys like Ozzie would take a nice girl like her, use her up and spit her out before she knew what had happened.

He took his skis, which Ozzie had off-loaded from the cart and planted in the snow, and hoisted them onto his shoulder.

Something flashed through Jacey's eyes. See? She was giving out signals that she didn't even know about! He told himself it was silly to adjust the skis with a completely unnecessary flex of his muscles—she couldn't even see them through his jacket!

Trevor realized with sudden urgency that these kind of thoughts had to be nipped in the bud. He had to get away from her. He had to clear his head. The morning had been way too intense. Something was going seriously off the rails here.

He deliberately removed his attention from her and turned toward the slopes. Something in him sighed. With utter relief.

Skiing. Nothing cleared a man's head like skiing. The immediacy of it. The required focus and strength. He glanced around and spotted the closest chairlift. He could ski there from where he was.

It was a weakness that he liked the idea of skiing over, showing off just a little for Jacey. He was a really good skier. A few perfect carved S curves would no doubt erase Ozzie's very juvenile cowboy maneuver with the cart from her mind. He set his skis on the ground and stepped into the binding. The click of it locking in place was satisfying.

"The ski instructor's name is Freddy," she said before Trevor even had the second ski on. She was squinting at the piece of paper Ozzie had given her. "I'll go in and find him. He probably needs to help fit me with equipment, right?"

Now some handsome guy was going to be floundering at her feet, helping her with boot fitting? Some stranger was going to be the one who saw her first moments on skis? Some stranger was going to be the one who witnessed her sense of wonder and discovery? Who saw her come alive, glow with inner light?

Reluctantly, he used his pole to release the binding. He stepped out of it.

"I think I'll take a lesson, too."

"What? You're an expert skier!"

"I've always wanted to try boarding."

"Really?"

No, that was a complete fib. He had never had the slightest interest in snowboarding, and yet he was astounded to find himself stepping away from his skis and opening the door to the ski school for her.

"Hi! Are you Jacey? I'm Freddy."

Trevor was inordinately relieved to see Jacey's ski instructor was a woman!

Until Jacey said, "This is my friend Trevor. He's decided he would like a boarding lesson."

"I'm not board certified," Freddy said, and then

giggled. "That makes me sound like a doctor, doesn't it? I think Bjorn is available, though."

Trevor should have considered this, that the boarding instructor and the ski instructor would be different people. So he wasn't going to be there with Jacey as she discovered the magic of skiing, after all. And he hadn't needed to protect her from overly zealous male attention.

This was the sad result of making impulsive decisions. If he'd done this in his engineering career, he wouldn't have a career!

He should just cancel, now, and go back to his original plan. Ski off, spend an hour or so alone while Jacey had her lesson, get his head on straight.

But then Jacey would know he'd been lying about wanting a boarding lesson, and he didn't want her to start wondering about his reasons for lying.

A perfect Swede—blond, blue-eyed, tall, muscled—swaggered out. It was exactly the instructor Trevor had dreaded Jacey getting. And so Trevor found himself signed up to do something he'd never had any intention of doing.

He wasn't aware, until he was on the snowboard, and it felt *awful*—like he was a duck trying to be a swan—how much he had planned on using his skill on the ski hill to protect Jacey. To be the one to introduce her to the wonder of the mountain. To maybe impress her just a little bit.

What did impressing her have to do with protecting her?

Maybe, if she was focused on him…

Crazy thinking, he told himself. Trevor was not used to crazy thoughts. At all. Or making a fool of himself.

And yet, here he was, on the bunny slope, entertaining crazy thoughts, and in full view of the whole world, making a complete fool of himself.

And somehow it felt as if it was all Jacey's fault!

But at least he could see her, and even from here, he could see the little furrow in her brow of mixed concentration and anxiety.

"Are you paying attention?" Bjorn asked sternly.

Oh, yeah, just not to Bjorn.

Jacey had low expectations of her ski lesson. She had never been either athletic or bold, and she assumed both qualities would be necessary for this sport.

And yet, she could see Trevor, just a few yards from her, and she had to admit she was glad he had stayed. It felt reassuring to have him close.

Somehow, having him close by also made it so she wouldn't give up if it was too scary or too hard.

What was that about? Why was she trying to win his approval?

She soon found out, though, that she couldn't focus on Trevor and learn to ski at the same time. She had to be entirely focused on herself.

After going through the rudimentary aspects of skiing, Freddy guided her to a baby lift: kind of like a giant black rubber carpet they could step onto with their skis on, and it transported them up the hill.

While on the *carpet*, the slope they were being transported up had seemed neither high nor steep, but standing at the top of it, it seemed both.

"Remember, beak over bindings," Freddy encouraged her. "A little bend, a little lean. Go!"

Jacey held her breath. She leaned forward and pushed a little with her poles. She thought it would be like being shot from a cannon, but no, it was slow. Still, she was going down the hill! She was skiing!

It lasted all of ten seconds until her tips crossed and she fell, but she was up in a heartbeat, and so ready to experience that *feeling* again.

Swooshing down that hill—even in slow motion—was wonderful.

By the end of her lesson, she could not believe how much fun she had had or how quickly the time had dissolved.

"Okay," Freddy said. "You did awesome. You're a natural."

She was covered in snow and her legs hurt but the sun was bright on her face and on the snow and she felt absolutely exhilarated by that, and by her accomplishments.

"For the rest of today stick to the Orion chair," Freddy said, pointing it out. "You can ski to it from here. It covers all the beginner's slopes. By the end of the day, you'll have a feel for it. And remember what I said about getting on and off the chairlift!"

The chairlift! A feeling tried to pierce her exhilaration, but then Trevor joined her, one foot on his board and the other off, pushing it.

The motion made him look extraordinarily powerful, but his expression was the antithesis of hers—dark, annoyed, frustrated.

"Freddy told me I'm ready for the chair!" she announced.

His frown softened slightly. "You looked like you were really enjoying yourself."

"I did. Didn't you?"

He rolled his shoulders. "It was okay."

"Well, I can't even explain what I'm feeling right now."

"I can see it," he said softly. "It's dancing like a light around you."

Was he leaning toward her? For one breathless moment, she felt as if he was going to touch her face.

Of course he wasn't going to touch her face! She had to quit entertaining these ridiculous notions. But she went very still, anyway, waiting to see what happened next.

What happened next was that the board scooted out from under him, his legs went akimbo and his rump went down into the snow.

"I'm going to change back into my skis," he said after lying there for a minute. Then he found his feet and got up. He did not look pleased about it as he swiped new snow off his jacket and his pants.

"Oh! I wish you wouldn't. I won't feel like such a loser if I have a partner in incompetence." She grinned at his expression when he heard the word *incompetence*.

What she really wanted, but couldn't quite find the words to explain, was for them to experience the *newness* of it together.

"How am I going to take care of you if I can barely stand up?"

"We'll take care of each other."

The statement shimmered in the air between them because wasn't that exactly what they were doing? Taking care of each other in this week so filled with terrible memories?

Caitlyn's little plan for them was evidently working. Because Jacey hadn't felt the weight of despondency since she and Trevor had arrived in Banff.

"Okay," he said reluctantly. "A couple of runs."

With a sigh, he pushed off in front of her. Despite the fact he was clearly more comfortable on skis, it was very easy to see that, unlike her, Trevor was a natural athlete, imbued with grace and power. In fact, by the time they reached the chairlift he seemed to have the rudiments of snowboarding completely conquered.

"You made that look really fun," she said, coming to a careful stop beside him.

"I think I may be starting to get the hang of it."

They moved into the lineup for the chair, and she basked in the sensations of it all: sun on her face, happy people around her, Trevor at her side.

"First time," she announced to the lift attendant when it was their turn to get on the chair.

"Quit saying that!"

The chair came up behind them. It caught her on the back of the knees and she sat with a graceless, sideways *thunk*, leaning into him.

"What? Why?"

"Guys are basically all evil-minded creatures, and I don't want to have to punch him if he asks about your virginal status."

She laughed. He glowered at her.

She debated telling him that getting on this chair was at least as terrifying as that other "first" had been in her life! But in the end, she decided that would be pushing the boundary of what was appropriate between them. She was aware she was blushing, anyway, just as if she'd said it.

The chair was gaining height rapidly. Her skis,

dangling at the ends of her feet, felt heavy, as if they might pull her over into the abyss.

"Bar coming down," he said.

She closed her eyes. "Bar? Thank goodness. Make mine a double. Margarita."

He chuckled. "Safety bar," he said and she opened her eyes to see him lowering a T-shaped bar between them. There was a place to rest her skis, and she felt infinitely safer.

"If you've made it this far without propping up your courage with a drink, I wouldn't suggest the ski hill as a great place to change."

"Sloppy drunk music teacher under your care on the ski hill!" she suggested, gleefully.

"No, thanks. How come you never told me you were thinking of giving it up?"

"Drinking?"

"Teaching music."

"It's not as if we've exchanged letters, Trevor."

"You confided your career plans in a complete stranger!"

"It came up!" she said and slid him a look. It was quite hilarious how he thought she was in some sort of danger of being bowled over by a bit of male attention.

"Well, since it came up, what's going on?"

Oh, sure, why not tell him about all her failures? It didn't even seem that important sitting here on the chairlift, high above a snow-covered world.

"I had the world's most promising student, and under my tutelage he failed the entrance audition to one of Canada's most auspicious music schools. It's shaken my confidence a bit. In the one area where I thought I had lots of confidence!"

"Hmmm."

"What's that mean?"

"Well, not enough confidence to perform in public. Even the lobby of the hotel seems to scare you."

"That's true," she agreed reluctantly. "Maybe Johnny's failure just exposed an insecurity I was already feeling. Anyway, maybe it's time for a break from music."

"But what would you do?"

She wasn't going to admit to Trevor the bazillionaire that she was thinking of getting a job at the corner grocery. He'd probably offer to buy her a company!

CHAPTER ELEVEN

"SOMETHING WILL COME UP," Jacey said, noncommittally.

Trevor looked thoughtful.

"That's why I think you need to think about it," he said. "You've had so much loss. Best friend. Husband. Home."

"It wasn't a home," Jacey corrected him. "It was a house. I didn't even like it that much."

"That's a pretty big investment in something you didn't like that much."

"Huh. Bruce's words, exactly. An investment." Why had she gone along with that huge financial commitment to a house she didn't even like? Oh, that was easy. She had been trying to win the unwinnable: Bruce's approval.

"I'm just saying that maybe it's just not the time to make a decision like that."

Jacey watched from her perch high above as the skiers swooped down the beautiful slopes of Moonbeam Mountain. It was a cold day, but the sun was so brilliant, it felt warm on her cheeks.

She could feel Trevor's shoulder up against hers, solid and providing her with a sense of safety and comfort, and something a little more. A sense of being physically in her body, wide-open to sensation, and there was plenty of that from where their shoulders touched.

Or maybe it was just the brand-new experience of skiing that had made her feel this tingling awareness of the physical.

Whatever it was—his shoulder touching hers or her first day on skis—it was providing her with that *something* that made pursuing a new adventure seem more exciting than terrifying.

Even from way up here, with nothing more than a skinny little barrier preventing her from slipping and falling to certain death. She leaned over the bar, better to see her skis dangling in space.

She sighed, drinking it all in, feeling a wonderful appreciation for the caprice of life. Even a few days ago, could she have ever envisaged this for her life?

A remote mountain ski hill, conquering her fear of heights, a gorgeous man beside her who *cared* about what decision she made next.

In the past, life taking abrupt or unexpected turns had never been a good thing.

And yet, she was aware of just feeling good.

"You're right," she told him.

"The words every man loves to hear," he said dryly.

"I should hold off on making the decision about my career. I'm going to do what I've heard other people talking about, but never quite managed for myself. I'm going to be totally in the moment, and embrace whatever life offers."

"Careful the offer isn't coming from someone like Ozzie. Or Bjorn."

"Who is Bjorn?"

"You didn't notice Bjorn?"

"Huh?"

"The Swedish man-god who taught snowboarding and took pleasure in torturing me on the slopes?"

She laughed. "Sorry, no."

And then she blushed. Because, really, not that she needed to let him know, but she'd barely noticed Ozzie, either.

Ozzie was on the periphery, was just part of the bigger picture, a world that she was excitedly sharing and exploring with Trevor. But even more, because of him. He was bringing out a bolder side of her.

Trevor looked pensive.

She was pretty sure they were both contemplating what it meant that she only had eyes for him.

And what this awareness of him, to the exclusion of all else, would mean to the temptations of trying out that hot tub tonight after an exhilarating—but muscle exhausting—day on the slopes.

Was he wondering that, too?

Still, she had to be careful of linking him too much to how she was feeling. It would be easy, with her life in tatters, to imagine there was the possibility of their friendship evolving into the kind of relationship hot tubs encouraged!

But somehow, even entertaining that thought, however briefly, felt disloyal to Caitlyn.

Thankfully, those thoughts were wiped from her mind as the next challenge presented itself: she had to get off the chairlift!

She managed to exit the lift area without face-planting, but then she and Trevor stood together at what felt like the very top of the mountain. It was gorgeous: an endless, snow-covered slope winding through exposed rocks, down to a place where huge timbers lined both sides of the wide run.

It was gorgeous, but hazardous. What if you lost control and hit one of those rocks? Or trees? Or another skier?

Despite Freddy's assurance that this was the novice run, it was no bunny slope! They couldn't even see the chairlift station at the bottom from here.

"Are you going to go?" he said.

She cast him a terrified look.

"It's kind of like having a baby," she told Trevor.

"You get to this point and have the sudden realization there's only one way out."

The faintest cloud passed over Trevor's face. She wished she wouldn't have mentioned babies.

That was how they had found out Caitlyn was sick—when she couldn't get pregnant.

Jacey gathered her strength. Why be afraid? The worst had already happened. She positioned her legs in a firm snowplow and planted her poles. She pushed.

It was steeper than the bunny hill had been. But still, she was in control. She did a careful turn across the hill as Trevor whizzed by her, all easy strength and confidence. She allowed herself to pick up speed.

It was exhilarating: the wind on her cheeks; the skis hissing on the snow underneath her; the sensation of freedom, almost of flying.

But then she realized she was going too fast and picking up speed despite her effort to dig deeper with her edges.

"Stop," she told herself. "Stop."

She realized she was yelling it out loud, and not stopping. She flew by Trevor. But then she heard him coming up behind her, trying to catch her.

She felt his hand on her jacket, grabbing for her, trying to slow her down.

But of course, it was impractical.

He was as new to snowboarding as she was to

skiing. With a shout, he lost his balance, and as he let her go she lost her balance, too.

They both tumbled until they came to a stop by crashing into each other. They lay there in the snow in a great tangled pile of limbs and equipment. Somehow, Trevor was on top of her, trying to keep his weight off her by holding himself up on his elbows.

She stared up at him. His curls were escaping from under his toque. She took in the beautiful sweep of his lashes, and the milk-chocolate color of his eyes. She noticed the whisker-shadowed cut of his jaw. She was so aware of the way his breath felt on her face, and how his body felt resting on top of hers. She could feel the strength in him, the warmth penetrating his jacket; she could even feel the steady beat of his heart.

She should have been cold, lying there with the snow at her back.

But instead, she felt as if she was on fire.

He took off his glove and brushed snow from her face. He looked down at her, his expression tender, as though bewildered as to how they had gotten here.

"Um, is that how they taught you to stop at ski school?" he asked, his voice a sensual growl.

"Falling over?"

"No, yelling 'stop' at the top of your lungs?"

She giggled. He chuckled. Her giggle turned to laughter and so did his. Here they were, all tangled together on the hill, doing the one thing it had felt as if they would never do again.

Laughing.

Uproariously.

Giving themselves over to it.

To the pure joy of unexpected and spontaneous moments.

The laughter died as Trevor suddenly seemed to become aware he was still lying on top of her and he rolled off her, then leaped up, held out his hand and pulled her back to standing. But he quickly let her go as soon as she had found her feet.

She guessed he had decided to act as if that close encounter of the best kind had never happened.

But the thing about something like that happening? No matter how much you pretended, it could never be the same again.

And it wasn't; the sizzle between them adding to the sensation of being totally free, as on fire with life as she had ever been. It was as if something in her that had been closed tight burst wide-open.

They never ended up on top of each other again, but that wide-open feeling remained. As she skied, Jacey let go a little and then a little more. She went faster. She fell. He went faster. He fell. But both of them were embracing their new skills, and the complete wonder of being part of the great outdoors, part of the mountain on a sun-drenched, brilliant winter day.

Their laughter and their shouts of exuberance echoed off the rocks and trees as they made their way down the run, and back onto the chair.

They sat, shoulder to shoulder, sharing brand-new things about each other that they had not revealed before, even though they had known each other for years.

He liked dogs. She liked cats. He liked rock and guitar, she liked classical and piano. He liked action movies, she liked drama. He liked traveling, she liked staying at home. She liked live theater, he liked live sports.

They stayed out on the slopes, taking run after run, until the lift attendant announced it was the last one of the day.

"Good thing it's the last run," Trevor said as she sat beside him on the chair. He threw his arm around her. They were both soaked from so many tumbles in the snow and she was shivering.

"It's funny," she told him. "I'm frozen, and I'm starving, and yet I still wish we had a few more chances to go down the hill."

"There's always tomorrow," he said.

When was the last time she had looked forward to the next day with such lovely anticipation?

"I can't wait," Jacey said. "Skiing is absolutely the most glorious thing I've ever experienced. I feel as if I've been missing out on something my entire life."

The frightening thing was it might have been skiing.

But equally, it could be *him*.

It could be the sensation of rocketing down that mountain hugging the edge of control, or it could just as easily be the sensation of ease mixed with exhilaration, confidence mixed with awkwardness, the feeling of getting to know someone deeply.

Friends, friends, friends, she told herself, but the mantra felt tiresome.

They were able to ski right to their hotel, and they left their equipment on the racks outside and raced each other in. Each of their bedrooms had its own en suite, and after they had showered they met again in the middle.

It felt dangerously intimate to be in this shared space.

"I'm starving," Jacey told him, eager to break the spell of Trevor, fresh from the shower, his hair curling sweetly and smelling like heaven. "Let's grab a hamburger."

"A hamburger? I don't think so. Moonbeam has some of the finest dining in the world, and we're availing ourselves of that."

She should insist on the hamburger. It would be just too easy to get used to this. To leading a life where money didn't matter, where all the best experiences were just laid out in front of you for the taking. How did you go back to macaroni and cheese after that?

On the other hand, why anticipate the future? Why not just surrender and enjoy the present?

"I'm not really dressed for anything fancy," she said, glancing down at her slim-fitting black yoga pants and white sweater.

His gaze skimmed her with such white-hot appreciation that she shivered, aware she was not the only one sensing the growing intimacy between them.

"One of the many joys of a mountain resort," he said. "You can five-star dine in your blue jeans."

He was wearing blue jeans, and a blue plaid shirt, open at the throat. It was unfair that a man could look so good wearing something so ordinary!

Trevor looked at Jacey across the table. They had chosen a small French restaurant and were seated at a window that overlooked the winding, snow-covered path of the village.

"It looks like a storybook," Jacey said.

Indeed, the village square, lit with gaslights, looked exactly like that. Golden light splashed out of windows under snow-laden roofs.

If he would have considered the general ambiance of French restaurants—the candlelight and roses thing—he might have opted for that hamburger.

Too late now.

Plus, he wasn't sure a hamburger would have brought about the same glow of happiness he was seeing now as she sampled the delights of coq au vin.

"I've never had food like this before," she said. "My dad and I kind of just squeaked by. And Bruce was, um, quite thrifty."

Trevor decided he didn't like Bruce, a lot.

CHAPTER TWELVE

"OH MY," JACEY SAID. She leaned back and savored her first bite of the next course. It was what the chef was famous for, boeuf bourguignon, served with homemade crusty bread. The stew was the perfect hearty dish to finish the day with.

Trevor thought the look of pleasure on her face was a look a man could die for. Bruce had missed this to save a few pennies? Men could be so dumb.

"I feel about this food the very same way I feel about skiing," she said. "As if I've missed something my entire life."

He was aware of feeling an urgent—and very dangerous—need to give Jacey every single thing she had ever missed.

Trevor told himself his desire to give Jacey everything she had never had before was motivated strictly by a desire to keep her away from losers like Bruce.

And Ozzie.

Once she'd seen how she should be treated, she

would never go back. He was quite pleased with the purity of his motive.

"What should we have for dessert?" Trevor asked Jacey. He was pretty sure every item on the dessert menu was something she had missed.

"I can't possibly have dessert."

He would not be thwarted.

"We can't possibly have a meal like that and not have dessert. We'll share something."

He asked the waiter for a recommendation, and they were brought a donut-shaped pastry filled with cream.

"Paris-Brest," the waiter announced with flourish.

"Why is it called that?" she whispered, and they both stared at it. She laughed first, and there it was between them, again.

The thing he had sworn—was it really less than twenty-four hours ago?—that he would never feel again.

Joy.

He took out his phone and looked up the dessert. "It's named after the region in France that it comes from."

She was blushing over the name of a dessert. He couldn't resist taking it a step further.

"Only the French," he said in a low tone intended only for her ears, "would name a whole region that."

"Get your mind out of the gutter," she said,

her tone also low. "It probably doesn't even mean that in French."

"We're talking about the people who named the Grand Tetons."

She laughed again, as he hoped she would. Ever since she had laughed this afternoon, he felt as if he could live for that sound.

He was enjoying their low tones—a couple sharing a secret joke. The gorgeous dessert had been presented with only one fork. Trevor realized sharing a dessert might not have been the best idea.

A dessert that made him think of breasts was an even worse idea, despite how much he'd enjoyed teasing her about it. Now it was making him think of him and Jacey tangled together on that slope, the way she had felt underneath him, tiny but supple.

He had to guard against *that* happening again even as he worked hard to give her great experiences.

Sharing Paris-Brest was obviously not forwarding that goal. They were eating off the same fork. She was holding it out to him; he was leaning into it.

"I think that may be the best thing I've ever tasted," Jacey decided.

She had said that about every dish. He steeled himself against the inevitable moment when she closed her eyes, and that low purr of pure plea-sure came from her throat.

It was true, though. It was the best dessert he'd ever eaten. But how much of that was because he imagined the taste of her lips remained on the fork?

He had to, of course, keep this from getting out of hand.

Tomorrow, Trevor decided, as a defensive mea-sure, he'd be on skis. That would put him in a better position to help her, without ending up on top of her. Plus, even while keeping his distance, there was the added benefit of being able to show her exactly what he could do.

How did showing off fit into his defensive plan?

They hadn't had any wine. It must be the food and the long day making him feel less sharp than normal.

Almost under a spell.

"I think I'll try snowboarding tomorrow," she decided halfway through dessert. "I'll take a les-son first thing in the morning."

He tried not to glare at her.

A lesson?

He was not leaving her—a woman who looked like that when she ate Paris-Brest—with a guy named Bjorn who, as competent as he was on a snowboard, obviously fell into the same category as her ex.

And her not so secret admirer, Ozzie.

"I'll take another boarding lesson, too," he said, saying a sad goodbye to the comfort of being on skis and wondering when exactly his life was going to get back on track.

But if the past years had been *on track* then maybe he could just embrace what was happening now.

Except for the hot tub.

He was not sure he had ever wanted anything quite as badly as to get into that hot tub when they got back to their suite. His muscles ached and the stars were out.

But Jacey in a bathing suit?

Had she even brought a bathing suit? He didn't recall seeing one in her suitcase.

It occurred to him this was the first time he'd be alone with a woman since Caitlyn. He realized, bewildered by how it had happened, that the evening had taken on a date feel.

He was pretty sure Caitlyn's plan for him involved him being a better man. Not falling for her friend!

Falling for Jacey?

Those kind of dangerous thoughts had to be nipped in the bud. Both he and Jacey had sustained hard lessons about love and loss. They were here to try and have fun. That was all. That was his entire mission: help Jacey have fun. Be a better man.

In the interest of the better-man part, after they had walked home through a village made more charming by darkness and warm lights burning behind closed windows, he claimed exhaustion and went straight to bed...where he tossed and turned and tried to decide if that look on her face, when he had said his abrupt good-night, had been disappointment or relief. The last time he checked the time it was 3 a.m.

Which probably explained why he felt so grumpy when he found himself outside the ski school the next morning with Bjorn ignoring him and absolutely beaming at Jacey.

"Aren't *you* the nicest surprise?" he asked, wagging those white-blond eyebrows at her and flashing perfect teeth.

Trevor Cooper was not an impulsive man. He was careful and meticulous. But in his defense, he was also exhausted.

That must have been why he put his arm around Jacey. She turned slightly toward him, her brow furrowed. Her look of surprise was going to completely ruin the deterrent effect of his possessiveness, so ever so casually, he planted a kiss on her lips.

Trevor had meant it only as a warning to Bjorn. *She's taken.*

But as soon as his lips touched hers, it felt as if the entire world, Moonbeam and Bjorn included, disappeared. Her lips were soft and inviting. She seemed so conventional, but Jacey tasted of wild things, honey and alpine flowers.

He'd intended the lightest touch to her lips but as she leaned into him and her lips parted, she kissed him back.

The tenderness—and the hunger—in her kiss, made him pull away, suddenly the one who was shocked. He tried to grasp all those noble ideas he'd had last night. It felt as if they were disappearing, fog closing around them, the sweet taste of her lips like sunshine after darkness.

"Honeymooners?" Bjorn asked, with good humor.

Trevor gave himself a mental shake, but his second snowboarding lesson was a disaster. He couldn't concentrate at all.

He'd kissed her strictly for her protection. Strictly.

But he felt shaken. He had never kissed anyone since Caitlyn. It felt wrong to have enjoyed it so much when it had been a mission-driven kiss, motivated absolutely for the right reasons!

Poor Jacey was naive in a sea where sharks swam. Caitlyn would have wanted him to protect her!

Jacey, who still wouldn't look at him, seemed to be concentrating just fine. In fact, she was doing way better on the snowboard than he was!

As soon as the lesson was over, Trevor headed for the chair without consulting her. He got on it and looked straight ahead as she settled beside him. Only then did he realize he was trapped. He hoped she'd be nice and pretend nothing had happened, but he was not so lucky.

"What was that all about?" she asked, her voice quiet.

"He seemed just a little too interested in you."

"Bjorn?" Her stunned tone told him he'd done the right thing. She didn't have a clue what men, including him, were like.

"You needn't act so surprised. Who else?"

"Let me get this straight," she said, her voice not quite so quiet now. "You kissed me, without my permission, to warn Bjorn away?"

"Exactly," he said, relieved she got his motive so clearly. "Normally, I would have asked your permission. But the circumstances were extenuating."

"They were not!"

"Aren't *you* the nicest surprise," he mimicked darkly. "I saw the look on his face."

"That's just insulting. You were marking me with a kiss, saying to Bjorn, *back off, she's mine*?"

"I might not have put it like that."

"Like what? A dog marking his territory by peeing on a tree?"

"I really wouldn't have put it like *that*."

"That's what it was."

"Okay, okay, I'm sorry. It didn't occur to me you might interpret it like that."

"My interpretation is the problem?"

Yes. He knew better than to say it out loud, though. He slid her a look. She was, unfortunately, really cute when she was mad. The taste of her lips, also unfortunately, seemed to be lingering on his own.

"Oh!" she said. "You saw his wedding ring, right?"

Trevor frowned. He hadn't actually seen that.

She started to laugh, but it wasn't a nice laugh at all.

"I'm afraid I fail to see what's funny."

"He's gay, Trevor."

"What? Bjorn?"

"Yes."

"How could you know something like that?"

"I saw him saying goodbye to his husband. They were standing outside Morning Sun Café, where we had breakfast."

Trevor had no right to feel so happy. The only thing that could make him feel happier than he felt right now was if Bjorn's husband was Ozzie.

He told himself his happiness was *protective* only. At least one of Jacey's unsuitable admirers had been eliminated. His *job* would be easier now.

But his happiness was short-lived.

"You know the real message you gave?" she asked him, her voice shaking with outrage. "That I'm not capable of making my own choices!"

"I said I was sorry."

"It wasn't heartfelt."

"Geez," he said. "Okay. In terms of your choices, there is Bruce to consider."

He pointed this out even though something was warning him now might not be exactly the time for his engineer's pragmatism to insist on backing his concerns for her with evidence.

"Bruce?" The quaver in her voice increased.

"Bruce, that guy you married who didn't support you through a tough time, who bought a house you didn't like and who was too cheap to take you out for a nice dinner. Ever."

Rather than being convinced by this very reasonable argument, her face went very red. It shouldn't have made her look cuter. But it did.

It shouldn't have made him want to kiss her again. Particularly since there was no one here to protect her from. But it did.

"I trusted you with that!" she sputtered.

It was a good thing they arrived at the top of the chairlift then because Trevor had the awful feeling she might have tried to push him off if she had to spend one more second with him.

Instead, Jacey cleared the chair with relative ease and whooshed off down the hill, never once glancing back, as if she had been riding that board her whole life.

Considering the level of confusion he was feeling right now, his motives and his mission weirdly muddy inside his own head, Trevor was glad to see her putting some much needed distance between them.

Why was she so angry? Jacey asked herself. The truth was that the overly protective part of Trevor was kind of endearing.

But the fact that he hadn't meant that kiss—at all—wasn't.

She had, embarrassingly, thrown herself into it! The terrible truth was she had found herself completely helpless against the primitive pull of his lips claiming hers.

And his cool assessment of her poor choice of a life partner hurt, probably even more so because it was true.

There had been warning signs about Bruce even before Caitlyn got sick. There had been the shoestring dates, the tiny ring, the budget wedding, the poor quality furniture choices. By the time they got to buying the house, Jacey had been well aware what she wanted placed a poor second—or maybe even third or fourth—in his consideration.

It made her so angry that Trevor saw all of that!

Still, the snow and learning the new skill forced her to focus hard on getting down the run in one piece.

That kiss, or maybe the anger—or some combination of both—seemed to heighten this experience. Snowboarding down the hill she felt an astonishing boldness. She felt extraordinarily aware—of her body and breath, and of how connected she was to the snow and the mountain through the vehicle of the snowboard.

It was everything Ujjayi had ever promised!

Intensity seemed to surge through her veins.

It felt as if it was a secret ingredient that had been missing from her life. Even before the death of Caitlyn, the failure of her marriage and Johnny's disastrous audition, this had been lacking from her.

This verve.

And then those life events, those disappointments, those heartaches, had dimmed her light even further.

Jacey got to the bottom of the run and glanced over her shoulder. She felt quite gleeful that Trevor was struggling with the snowboard. Even with his natural athleticism, he was obviously having difficulty with transferring a lifetime of doing things one way to a brand-new way of doing them.

She got on the chairlift by herself. Without him! Without anyone. And it felt absolutely awesome!

She did another run by herself, and then another. But it finally occurred to her that Trevor appeared to be avoiding her, too. Was he *glad* they weren't skiing together?

CHAPTER THIRTEEN

Jacey squinted up the mountain. Trevor was a few minutes behind her. She could get on the lift without him. She could board all day without him.

But he was missing her transformation into a person who was powerful and independent. She wanted him to witness that.

So that the next time he kissed her, it would be because he wanted to, not because he had some archaic notion that it was up to him to ride in on a white stallion and save her from a lifetime habit of making bad choices!

The next time?

Oh, yeah. There was going to be a next time, and it was not going to be his choice at all. The next time the decision would be made by the newly empowered Jacey Tremblay!

Reality burst the bubble of her moment of empowerment.

What would Caitlyn think about Jacey's desire to kiss her husband? Was making a plan to kiss Trevor the right thing?

She frowned and thought of that letter.

Two years.

They had been drawn together by Caitlyn's own hand. Trevor said his wife had suspected Jacey's own marriage was in trouble.

Could her friend have possibly guessed they would both be single? Certainly, she would have known Trevor well enough to know he wouldn't move on easily.

You're being crazy, Jacey told herself, uneasily. Her best friend was not match-making from heaven.

And yet, she remembered, suddenly, lying on the banks of the Bow River the morning after Caitlyn's bridal shower. It had been a beautiful spring day, and coming from out of town, Jacey had stayed with her friend. They had walked down to the nearby river, coffees in hand and, exhausted from all the shower shenanigans, had lain on their backs on the grassy slope, knees up and arms folded over their tummies.

"I love your happiness," Jacey had said to her.

And she had said, so softly, "I wish there were two of him so we both could marry him."

By bringing them together for this trip, had Caitlyn put her stamp of approval on what might unfold? Drawing in a deep breath, Jacey made her decision.

She waited for him to get on the lift with her

and didn't move away from the pressure of his shoulder.

"Are you going to be mad all day?" he asked, not realizing she wasn't mad at all anymore, but the enormity of the decision she had just made had rendered her to silence.

"Because you're spoiling it," he said quietly.

"I'm spoiling it?" But she turned her head and looked at him. Really looked at him. He looked exhausted. He'd already said he hadn't slept last night.

If she was going to be a woman worthy of the man who had loved Caitlyn, she could not make it all about herself.

Helping each other—emotional complexities aside—was the reason they were here.

Caitlyn had been bang-on sending them here. They certainly hadn't been wallowing in the sadness of the anniversary that had just passed.

She touched his arm. "Let's not spoil it," she said. "You're right."

"The words every man loves to hear," he reminded her.

And then he smiled. And the sun seemed to shine even more brightly in her world.

With the tension eased between them, they snowboarded all day. They embraced the simple pleasures of new challenges, being outside, exerting themselves. Both of them gained confidence and after lunch they moved off the Orion chair and onto the Big Dipper.

"Last run," the liftie told them as he guided the chair to them.

"I can't believe it's the last run already," Jacey said, leaning into the back of the chair, breathing deeply of the fresh mountain air. "Part of me is glad. My muscles are screaming, *no more*, and part of me is so sad."

"We have tomorrow."

That made her feel even sadder. That only tomorrow was left. Would she be brave enough to kiss him again, to follow her heart where it wanted to go? The time seemed too tiny to explore the feelings building in her like the clouds on top of that mountain.

"We can ski out tomorrow afternoon. I am definitely skiing instead tomorrow."

It was *love vs. bathrooms* again! She was thinking of romantic possibilities; he was planning his ski day.

Maybe they were miles apart. Maybe there was a chasm between them that could not be crossed.

"I like boarding," Trevor said, "but I have a man's natural tendency to show off what I can really do."

He wanted to show off *for her*. Maybe the chasms were not so deep and wide as she thought. She felt herself looking at his lips. She had experienced what he could really do!

"You'll love skiing out," Trevor told her. "Or boarding."

"I don't even know what that means."

"We can send our luggage on the gondola and we can ski down. It's a really long run. I'd have to look it up, but maybe the longest in the world."

"I'm glad it's going to be ending on that note," she said. "Because I'm really sorry it's ending. I have had the best time."

He gazed down at her. "Me, too."

"I'm so glad."

"Caitlyn was right. I should have known she would be. She was always right."

"Women generally are," she said, straight-faced.

"Says the one who took the wrong turn up there on Merak that nearly took us off a cliff."

"Says the one who decided he was ready to take air and I followed him off a jump!"

"You loved it."

"Everyone says that when they survive."

"Anyway, it's not over yet. Let's go find something to eat."

And so they ate. Hamburgers tonight, because they were both too hungry to go back to the hotel and change. And far too hungry to wait for really good food to be prepared.

When they came out of the restaurant, it was dark.

"It feels like it's warming up," Trevor said. He

stopped and sniffed the air. "I wouldn't be surprised if it's snowing by morning."

After that day of chasing each other down Moonbeam Mountain, after the truce, Jacey was aware she was still being consumed by the memory of that kiss.

There was some trembling kind of awareness of him inside her, made sharper by this wolflike sniffing of the air, the prediction of flurries.

He leaned over and scooped up a handful of snow. He made it into a ball. "See? It's getting sticky."

"Like snowball-fight sticky?"

"Grow up," he said, sternly.

Hurt, she marched ahead of him. The snowball hit her in the middle of her back. She turned around and he shouted with laughter and dashed away.

She gathered up some snow and formed it into a missile.

"I have the right gloves for this," she warned him. "I'm not giving up until you surrender."

A childlike joy shimmered in the air between them as they chased each other through the main square of the village, screeching with laughter and tossing snowballs at each other until they were shivering and soaked.

"My hands are freezing despite the gloves," she told him, finally, puffing with exertion and laughter. "And my legs are killing me. They feel as if they're turning to mush."

He came and stood in front of her.

She gazed up at him, at the darkness of his eyes, at the fullness of the lips she had tasted.

"Okay," she whispered, "I surrender."

Without taking his gaze from hers, he reached for her hands, took off her gloves one by one and shoved them into his pockets.

And then he lifted her frozen hands to his lips, and he blew on them.

Maybe she had led a sheltered life—okay, she *had* led a sheltered life—but Jacey was pretty sure that Trevor blowing his warm breath on her cold hands on a starlit night in Moonbeam Village was just about the sexiest thing that had ever happened to her.

She had told herself the next kiss would be her choice. She pulled free of where his hands had cupped hers, and she leaned into him. She took his face in between her hands. She had to stand on her tiptoes.

She kissed him.

She kissed him with all that she had learned about herself that day. She kissed him with boldness, embracing the incredible sensation of giving herself over, completely.

She lost herself in his kiss, in the wash of glory

that came from sharing such an incredible intimacy with him.

She lost herself. But found herself, too.

Trevor pulled away from Jacey and took her in.

Moonbeam was living up to its name at the moment; the entire mountain and village bathed in silvery light.

Jacey's face, illuminated by that light, was absolutely gorgeous. All day he'd been noticing something about her, something new, shimmering in the air, electrical.

In the moonlight it became crystal clear to him what that was.

Passion, he realized. She was unleashing the side of herself he'd seen hints of in the color of the suitcase, in the way she'd been drawn to the spectacular jacket she was wearing now.

He realized he really should have thought it through. Before he had opened this door by kissing her this morning.

Had his motivation really been about protecting her? He'd tried to convince himself of that all day. Or had he, as men were apt to do, cloaked a selfish motive in one that seemed more virtuous?

Tasting her so fully now, he felt as if he knew himself, and as if that knowing told him a deep truth.

He had wanted to taste her.

He had wanted this moment when they both surrendered.

Looking back, the moment it had all started to shift was when they had gotten on the gondola together. He had glimpsed it then.

Who she really was, that ability to move past fear, to grow from it, to allow it to change her.

And now, as they had explored the whole mountain, laughing, filled with the spirit of adventure, sat, shoulder to shoulder, discovering different runs and different chairs, and each other; now that they had sampled dessert from a shared fork, who she really was was so apparent he could not believe he had ever missed it.

He should have really thought this through before blowing on her hands on a moonlit night on the mountain.

The temptation of knowing her even more rose in him. He could picture them together in that hot tub.

It was the natural conclusion for this day. The only fitting conclusion.

But where was all this going?

He had to think about that. It was Caitlyn's doing that they were here. She had entrusted him with the well-being of her best friend.

He had to get his head screwed back on straight. He had to remember he and Jacey were both in an altered state up here.

So removed from the real world.

So intensely aware of each other.

He just had to be strong. It was just for one more night. He just had to do the right thing—be the better man—for just one more night.

"I was thinking the hot tub might be nice," she said softly.

It was as though she was reading his mind. Knowing his weakness.

He thought how angry he had made her kissing her this morning. But it hadn't really been anger; it had been hurt.

And he saw how much worse he could hurt her now.

"I'm allergic," he blurted.

She was scanning his face.

"The chemicals," he expanded.

Her look of disappointment was crushing.

"I get a rash."

"Oh. We could watch a movie."

"No, no. I wouldn't deprive you. You go ahead. I'll see you in the morning."

And he raced to his room and shut the door before his nose grew ten inches or his pants caught on fire.

He heard her softly open the patio door a few minutes later; heard her pad through the snow on the deck. Could a man hear a towel whisper off? He could certainly hear the gentle splash as she got in the water.

He wondered what the hell she was wearing.

He was pretty sure she didn't have a bathing suit. Her underwear?

Naked?

She wouldn't be that bold, would she? Well, the woman who had arrived at his doorstep a few days ago might not have been.

But the woman who had led the charge down the very tricky Phecda run would certainly be bold enough to step into a hot tub under a starlit night in the altogether.

He contemplated that with some agitation.

As it turned out, you didn't have to be a liar to have pants on fire!

Even long after she'd abandoned the hot tub and gone to bed, Trevor lay awake, tossing and turning, his second night without sleep.

It was a good thing they were leaving tomorrow because he was not sure he could be held responsible, in close proximity to a hot tub, for what a sleep-deprived man could be capable of.

CHAPTER FOURTEEN

JACEY FELT HER physical aches and pains dissolve into the gorgeous hot water. The emotional aches and pains were not so easy to dissolve.

She leaned back and studied the stars through the veil of steam. She felt deeply mortified.

Was Trevor really allergic?

He had shut down the suggestion of the movie, too. So the embarrassing truth was her newfound boldness had been met with rejection.

He probably thought she was a terrible friend to Caitlyn.

Maybe she *was* a terrible friend to Caitlyn, reading way too much into Caitlyn's last wish for them both.

Jacey had no doubt what would have unfolded if they got in the hot tub together.

The air between them tonight had been electric with sensuality. With *wanting* each other.

But that step between them was a huge one, complicated by their past relationship. By their mutual love of Caitlyn. By their mutual loyalty to her.

Jacey suspected Trevor had once again been casting himself in a protective role. He was putting on the brakes before they did something they both regretted.

But would she regret it?

At the moment it didn't feel as if she would have. She felt she was aching with unfilled need. Still, while it was all well and good to be bold, sometimes there were consequences; sometimes the genie could not be put back in the bottle once it had been allowed out.

And it didn't matter if she didn't regret it if he did! It was possible they were having two entirely different experiences.

It was then Jacey realized it was not just *need* that she was feeling.

It went far deeper than that.

It was true the past few days had allowed her to know Trevor better, and on a different playing field.

But she had known him for a very long time. She realized that she felt as if she now knew Trevor *deeply.*

Some terrible awareness wiggled to life inside her.

The most dangerous thing of all had happened while she was out playing in the snow, letting go, being emboldened by life.

It wasn't just that those things were making

her feel so alive, so on fire with life, so intense, so engaged.

Not by a long shot.

She was falling in love with Trevor. Maybe she even had been in love with him for a long, long time.

She had seen him go through the most devastating moments of his life, and how he had not broken—even if he thought he had. She had watched his incredible strength be tested and tried beyond what most men could endure.

He had shown her what real love looked like.

Perhaps it was in those moments—of his courage, of his selflessness—that she had known her own marriage was beyond repair.

"Caitlyn," she asked the inky night, "what do you think of all this? What if I started to love your husband even before you died?"

Her question was met with the deep silence of the dark mountain night.

She realized she was crying.

"I feel horrible," she whispered, "A horrible friend, a horrible person. Trevor probably knows how horrible I am. I'm so mixed up. I don't know good from bad at the moment."

There was no magic at all in the hot tub or in the mountain night. She got out and felt the sting of cold on her wet skin. The whole world suddenly felt jumbled, confusing, terrifying.

In retrospect, Jacey realized she had done nothing but make mistakes in love her entire life. Craving it so badly. Needing to bask in the unconditional approval only love could bring.

She realized she was glad he had put the brakes on, as humiliating as that was. She didn't want what she was feeling for Trevor to be tested.

She wanted to enshrine it.

And she never, ever wanted him to know.

When Trevor got up in the morning, the first thing he saw was that the snow he had predicted had arrived through the night.

Looking out his window, he realized the snow was coming down so hard he could not see across the village square, let alone to the peak of Moonbeam.

The second thing he noticed was the underwear Jacey had worn in the hot tub last night was draped over the towel bar in the bathroom. Red. And lacy.

Surprising secrets. Something white-hot threatened to sear him.

But when she emerged from her own room she seemed, thankfully, distant. One thing she was not was stupid. She had realized he wasn't really allergic to the hot tub and she would have read that as rejection, which he was sorry for. But he'd already let things get way out of hand. She would thank him for it one day.

But that day wasn't today.

It wasn't that she wasn't polite. Cordial even. But there was something guarded in her—and in him. The connection was gone between them, and he missed it.

They packed their things in silence—her undies disappeared off the towel bar—and put their suitcases by the door to be picked up and brought down to the parking lot for them after they had skied out later in the day.

She looked at her phone through breakfast. It was the first time he'd seen the phone since she had taken photos at the Banff gates. It made him aware of how in the moment she had been—they both had been—that neither of them had used their phones at all in the past two days.

He was a little sorry—and a little relieved—that she was using it now. And that it was doing exactly what those devices did.

Locking him out of her world. Putting distance between them.

"Just checking my flight," she said, glancing up at him. "We'll be back in Calgary in plenty of time to get me to the airport, right? It goes at eight."

"You're leaving tonight?"

He had thought she would spend the night back at his house. He was aware he wanted that, even as he dreaded it.

She glanced up at him.

He realized then that she wasn't checking her flight; she was changing it.

As she withdrew from him, he felt an aching loneliness open inside him. It shocked him how deeply he yearned for her company, to re-create the feeling of connection between them.

But he knew he needed to be strong just a little bit longer.

They were on the mountain all day, despite the storm absolutely buffeting them. He skied rather than trying the snowboard again, but he had lost his desire to show off for her, to draw her further into the dangerous game they had been playing.

When they shared the chair on the lift he noticed, despite the fact it would have given them both comfort from the storm, she sat squished against the far edge, avoiding touching his shoulder. Conversation was limited by the howling of the wind.

There were other storms brewing that they needed protecting against.

Finally, it was over. He, coming off another sleepless night, was exhausted by the effort of subduing all the things that had been developing between them.

"Are you ready to ski out?" he asked her.

Are you ready for it to be over?

She nodded, not meeting his eyes.

He took the map of the resort from his zipped jacket pocket. He'd skied out before, but in the storm he thought the entrance to the Galaxy Trail might be tricky to find. The wind nearly tore the map from his hands.

Just as they arrived at the trailhead, an attendant was swinging a huge gate shut. In French and English a sign declared the trail closed.

"I'm supposed to get the word out," the resort employee said. "There's been an emergency. Everyone is supposed to gather in the lobby of Moonbeam Manor. There will be an announcement."

They skied down to the nearest chair, rode back up and made their way through the deepening storm back to Moonbeam.

The huge lobby now had dozens of people milling about. When it seemed not another person could squeeze in, a manager held up his hand and silence fell.

"I'm afraid there's been an avalanche," he said solemnly. "The access road that leads from the highway to the parking lot has been completely covered. We'll have it fixed as soon as possible but meanwhile, we are snowed in."

There was a collective gasp from the gathering.

"No need to worry," he assured them. "We're completely prepared for all the surprises Mother Nature throws at us. This isn't the first time this has happened, and it won't be the last. Those of you who were expecting to leave us today have been put back in your rooms, as guests who should have been arriving will not be coming.

"There will also be a complimentary bar and a buffet dinner set up here—" he glanced at his watch "—in just a few minutes. Thank you for your patience with us and Mother Nature."

Trevor and Jacey went back to their room, then showered and changed and went down to the dinner. They exchanged a few polite words about the turn of events, but Trevor noticed how stilted they were with each other. He longed to knock down the wall around Jacey, at the very same time that he wanted to leave it where it was. He was a man at war with himself.

There was actually quite a festive, almost party atmosphere in the lobby. The buffet was out and the drinks were flowing. A fire roared in the hearth.

Bjorn was there and came over to introduce them to his husband, Jasper.

Trevor noticed that despite the charm and humor of the two men, Jacey still seemed distant.

"You know what we need? A good old sing-along! Can you imagine? The fire roaring, the snow outside, voices raised. Does someone know how to play that piano?" Jasper asked.

Bjorn looked at him indulgently. "Life is not 'White Christmas,'" he chided his partner.

"I know how to play," Jacey said.

Trevor shot her a look. She didn't meet his gaze.

Instead, she took Jasper over to the piano and sat at the bench. "What would you like me to play?"

"Let's start with a round song!" Jasper said, delighted. This was obviously his forte. He quickly had the people divided into two groups. After his instructions, he signaled Jacey.

Gamely, she accompanied his "Row Row Row Your Boat."

Trevor watched her, frowning. Jacey did not seem to him like someone facing her greatest fear.

He thought of the way she had been today, withdrawn, cold. He felt stricken. He had caused that. Caused this. Now this woman was facing her greatest fear, not because she had found herself, but because she had risked something, been rejected and now felt as if she had nothing left to lose.

Bjorn had joined Jasper. The pair of them had amazing voices and were natural entertainers.

Jacey could play every single request they threw at her. Casually, as if her fingers flying across that keyboard was without effort. Making music happen was as natural to her as breathing.

Then one of the other staff members came over to Bjorn and said something in his ear. He went very still. He held up his hand and Jacey stopped playing.

"It seems," Bjorn said, addressing the crowd,

"that they can't find Ozzie. He left early today. He's recorded as going down on the gondola."

Complete silence replaced joy. Where there had been festiveness, now there were growing whispers of anxiety and worry.

"There are search crews out right now," Bjorn said. "They will find him." He nudged Jacey. "Play something!"

She went very still. She glanced at the people gathered. It was almost as if she came awake in that moment and realized exactly what she was doing.

Trevor saw in her face the moment hope won. That she went from *nothing to lose* to somehow who she really was.

Her spine straightened. Her fingers were poised over the keys.

And then she took a deep breath. She closed her eyes. When she opened them, it was as if she was alone in that crowded room. She began to play.

Slowly, as she played, the anxious whispers faded and silence fell over the room. Trevor had never heard music like that, and from the rapt silence in the room, he was pretty sure no one else ever had, either.

Phones came out, people recording her, understanding what they were hearing was a once-in-a-lifetime—if that—experience.

Jacey, looking so ordinary sitting there in jeans

and a sweater, became something that was not ordinary at all.

She became the music.

It was incredible. Every single thing it was to be human was in every note. All sadness, all joy, all sorrow, all triumph. The music soared and fell and soared again.

He saw this was the gift she was giving them; all of them. Jacey, through her music, was going to a place mere words could never go. She was telling them the story of life.

But she was also telling them the story of herself.

Trevor saw every single thing she was. He could see the same quiet courage and resolve he had seen when she would not leave the side of her dying friend, even when it meant her own life was going to be left in shambles.

You could not hear that music and not know who she was.

Her soul was exposed to all of them.

The music wound down, ending finally on a single note that carried on and on like the sob of a woman who had lost her child.

When the note ended, absolute stillness followed. It stretched, and stretched some more, and then someone began to clap, and then the clapping was thunderous.

Somebody called, "Encore."

And others took up the chant.

It felt as if he, alone, in that entire room, could see that Jacey had nothing left. He saw that she was suddenly aware of having exposed herself, of being wide-open to strangers. People were surging toward her. Asking questions, thanking her, but Trevor moved through the crowd, knowing now was the time, if ever there had been one, that Jacey genuinely needed his protection.

She saw him coming, and for the first time that day, they connected. Her eyes met his, she leaned toward him and her face lit up with relief.

And something else that he couldn't quite put his finger on but that warmed him to his core.

He helped her gently off the bench, and the applause started again. He put her under the protection of his arm and acted as a shield as he quickly got her out of the room.

The door separating the main from the hallway whispered shut, but they could still hear the applause. And then, finally, silence.

He heard someone shout into the new silence, "Ozzie's been located. He's okay."

CHAPTER FIFTEEN

JACEY SAGGED. WITHOUT HESITATING, Trevor put one arm under her knees and the other behind her shoulders and scooped her up against his chest.

She sighed her relief, her breath forming a puddle of warmth that expanded with her every breath, until it seemed to envelop him.

Inside the safety of their suite, he set her down with an exquisite tenderness that he had not known he was capable of.

She was actually shaking, like someone in shock. She looked at him, her face pale, those green eyes, so familiar, resting on him with an expression of trust a man could live for.

"I'm sorry," she whispered. "I feel so emotional."

"Because Ozzie's been found?" He realized that niggle of jealousy was gone, completely erased by the look in her eyes.

"Yes, that, too."

"But?"

"It's that piece of music. I've been working on it for a long time. I've never played it in its entirety before. Even then, I played it by myself. And for myself."

"You composed that?"

She nodded. "I did."

"Wow."

She hesitated. "It's Caitlyn's song."

And then he understood. The life and death he'd heard in every note. Sweetness and sorrow. Love and loss. Residing side by side.

It was the whole story of what it was to be human.

Like a man who had been stumbling through the wilderness and had found a shelter, a welcoming light glowing from within, he came home to her.

He embraced all of it.

He embraced her.

He realized he had used all his strength to postpone a moment that could no more be stopped by such a puny thing as human will than that avalanche that had roared down the mountain.

His lips found hers and told her, as words could not, that he saw her. That he saw her completely.

And that he needed her like that, too.

Completely.

Jacey's bones felt as if they had turned to water, even before Trevor's lips sought hers. Found hers. Claimed hers.

Jacey had never experienced her own music

in the way that she just had. Her music had been missing all the things her life had been missing.

The intensity. The passion. She knew, somehow, that piece of music had been waiting for the perfect moment, for that secret ingredient.

And so had she. Jacey had never been more aware of that than when she twined her arms around the strong column of Trevor's neck. It felt as if her whole life had been moving toward this moment.

Wholeness.

Her lips parted under the gentle command of his. She thought the snowboarding and the mountain had shown her everything there was to know about living with intensity.

But now that assumption felt laughable.

This was intensity. The exquisite taste of Trevor, the rippling sensations that shivered through her as he took the kiss longer and deeper, as his hands tangled in the wisps of her short hair, as he pulled her closer into him. She was so close to him, in fact, she could feel the beat of his heart. She was so close to him it felt as if the heat coming off his skin could singe her.

His body was incredible, hard, taut, muscular. She had seen that in him, always, in the way clothes flattered his masculinity, in the way he carried himself, with the easy confidence of a man who was at home in himself and sure of his own strength.

But today, when Trevor had chosen skis instead of the snowboard, it felt as if every nerve in her body had quivered with even more awareness of him. He skied with a grace that seemed unearthly, his great strength blending with snow and rock, mountain and sky, to create a powerful ballet.

Was it because he had chosen to ski that Jacey's awareness had been so painfully heightened? Or was it because she had acknowledged, finally, to herself, how deeply her feelings ran for him?

It had made her greedy for the sight of him, even as she tried, all day, desperately, to hide that greediness, that *wanting*, from him. Being careful not to touch him, hardly engaging, trying not to look at his eyes or his mouth, or his hands.

But now, here they were. She was being confronted with everything that she had secretly felt and fought as they experienced the storm-enshrouded slopes of Moonbeam—the longing, the need, the hunger.

She was aware she could fight no more. Her strength was gone from her. Used up by a day of fighting herself, whatever remnants that remained, used up by the music.

It seemed like a very long time ago that she had arrived at Trevor's house and he had thrown open that door, aggrieved. Without his shirt on, those pajama bottoms clinging to the jut of his hips. Honestly, if she thought about it, she had been both longing for—and fighting—this moment ever since then.

Maybe even long before then.

Trembling, she reached for the buttons on his shirt. She undid them, one by one, slid her hands inside and touched the heated surface of his skin.

He went very still as she explored him. Again, she was aware that what she had understood to be intensity on the mountain paled in comparison to this. Even that feeling she had when she played the piano—immersed, lost in another world— paled in comparison to this sensation.

She was filled to the top and then to overflowing by the heated warmth of his skin, tight and warm, silky and smooth. Her fingertips played over his ribs and belly, over the hard buttons of his nipples.

With a low moan of both pleasure and pain, he finally stilled her hands, capturing them with his own. Holding her hands to his chest, Trevor retook her lips.

There was nothing left of gentleness in his kiss.

His lips captured. They plundered. They took. They demanded.

When he scooped her up in his arms again and strode across the suite, kicking open his bedroom door, she knew she was his captive.

That she was the maiden and he was the warrior. He put her down on the bed. He stared down at her, his eyes dark with hunger, with wanting, with appreciation, with *knowing*.

And Jacey was certain that there had never, in the entire history of the world, been a captive as willing as her.

He took off his shirt with tantalizing slowness. And then his slacks dropped to the floor, and he stood before her, gloriously male, so beautiful it hurt to look at him without touching him.

She opened her arms to him and he came and laid himself tenderly on top of her, the sensation of his naked chest burning her through her blouse. The trail of fire continued as his lips touched her cheeks, her chin, her neck, and then dipped lower.

Without taking his lips from her, adding to the sensation by flicking her skin with his tongue, his hands dispensed buttons, removed her arms from sleeves. And then, with a snap of his wrist, her bra was open and then gone. They were heated flesh to heated flesh. The fire was now like a volcanic lake, so intense it felt as if it could consume everything around it.

He backed off from that consuming intensity, gazing at her with wonder and delight. And then he surged forward. He teased her. She tormented him. He nipped. She nibbled.

They were captive, not just to each other but also to something bigger than them both.

A force of nature that put the storm outside to

shame, that commanded them both to finally, finally, finally surrender.

The sweetest surrender of all, a climb to the very top of a mountain, a moment balanced on the precipice.

And then the leap.

Not to fall.

No, to fly.

And then to find earth, to climb the mountain and to fly again.

All night they explored and experimented; they discovered and delighted in each other. Finally, beyond exhausted, their bodies tangled together, they slept the deep sleep of the utterly satiated.

And yet, in the morning, the hunger—the desire to climb to the top of the mountain—was back, as if it had never been slaked at all. And they began again.

The storm lifted at noon, about the same time they came up for air.

When they went and found a place to eat, they discovered the access road remained closed.

The resort had seemed a place separate from the world even before it had been cut off completely. But now it felt like their private playground. As the sun broke through the clouds, they decided to tackle the slopes for the afternoon.

Jacey was not sure she had ever felt the kind of exhilaration that coursed through her veins as she followed Trevor down Man in the Moon, her first black diamond, the ski run that required the most skill.

With the wind in her hair, the sun on her face and her *lover* leading the way, she was aware her body had never felt so exquisitely and completely alive.

And when she made it to the bottom without a single fall, and he threw his arm around her and kissed her on the mouth, it was bliss.

Pure bliss.

He lifted his head from hers. "Do you hear that?"

"No. What?"

"I think the gondola is running."

She cocked her head toward the sound.

"It means the access road had reopened."

She considered this with a sinking heart. Somehow, she had thought maybe they had days to investigate each other completely, not hours. Bliss notwithstanding, it felt as if they had wasted time skiing!

"Race you back to our room," she challenged him.

And with the mountains ringing with their laughter and shouts, they found their way back to privacy, back to each other's arms one more time before they had to leave their magical kingdom behind.

With a fire in the hearth and darkness falling

they made slow, soft, beautiful love on the floor in front of it.

Poised above him, after the loving, looking at his face, made more gorgeous by the flickering light of the fire, Jacey felt everything within her go still.

She realized it wasn't intensity that had allowed her to give birth to Caitlyn's song after such a long period of gestation.

Intensity had only been one element of a larger truth.

The truth she had been trying so desperately to distance herself from when an avalanche had forced her hand.

Love was the secret ingredient.

Love.

"Love."

She said it out loud this time, consciously. The word felt glorious, rich and full.

"I love you," she said, her voice low, brimming with the truth she was revealing to him.

She wanted to say more—so much more—that maybe she had loved him for a long time. That maybe Caitlyn had *wanted* this for them. That they should love again. That he was everything she could have ever hoped for in a lover: strong, considerate, passionate, beautiful—

But it pierced her euphoria that his expression had changed and she clamped her mouth shut before *all* of it spilled out of her.

If there was one look a woman did not want to see on a man's face after she had uttered her declaration of love to him, it was *that* one.

Regret.

Even before he spoke, she knew what he was going to say.

"I can't."

Slowly, regally, she untangled herself from him.

"You can't?" she asked him, and heard the leashed fury in her tone. "You can't what?"

He was silent.

"You can't what?" she insisted. "Say it back? Love me as much as I love you? Go forward? Have me in your life?"

Just barely, she managed to bite her tongue before she added, "You can't get over Caitlyn? Love me as much as you loved her?"

Looking at him, her fury grew.

"You don't mean *can't*," she accused him, jumping from the bed. "What you really mean is *won't*."

"That's not—"

She held up her hand. "Save it. You know what I just realized? I gave you everything. I trusted you with my every single fear and vulnerability. I trusted you with *me*. And what did I get from you? Nothing!"

She stormed into the shower. But then the fury died as quickly as it had come, and the power of it was replaced with something much worse.

She could feel her heart shattering, breaking into a billion pieces with the helpless realization that Trevor was not in the same place as she was.

He was not feeling the same things she was.

It was that devastatingly simple.

When she came out of the shower, he was in his room, behind closed doors. She could hear the hiss of his shower running; picture the water on his skin. Her mind slid there, tormented.

Revisited the pure sensuality of steam and heat and skin made slippery by soap, by lips tasting, touching *everywhere*.

The thoughts made her so weak with longing she wondered if it was possible to survive.

Of course it was possible to survive! She had an intimate knowledge of surviving disappointment.

Her whole life had really been preparing her for *this*.

Somehow, she managed to leave the hotel with him, to sit beside him in embarrassed silence as the go-cart delivered them to the gondola. It was full dark as they rode it down, but even if it had been light, all the enchantment of the first time—of overcoming her fear—was now overshadowed by the humiliation of not being loved back.

To his credit, he didn't try to say anything. Not. One. Single. Word.

But his expression of guilt—as if he was

ashamed of himself—only made everything so much worse.

His vehicle was covered by a mountain of fresh snow.

Only yesterday she would have helped him clean it off. They would have been a team. A snowball fight might have broken out. Or a spate of cold-lip kisses.

Today she got in when he opened the door.

He got in his side and started the engine so that she would be warm while he swept away snow and scraped at icy windows.

She hated it that he was being chivalrous. It would be so much easier if he was a jerk.

Finally, they were ready to go. They got a short distance down the access road when they came to the place the avalanche had come down across it.

One lane had been plowed clear through a debris field, huge walls of snow rising on either side of it.

The headlights of the vehicle starkly illuminated the destruction. The absolute and furious power of the avalanche was so apparent. What had once been a solid road was churned up into the snow. It was as gray and wet-looking as freshly poured concrete.

Huge trees had been violently snapped in half and were embedded in the wall of snow, and a little farther down a root ball from what must have been a gigantic tree stuck out, the roots bare and tangled.

The avalanche felt like the perfect metaphor for Jacey falling in love with Trevor. It, too, had been a force of nature. It, too, had seemed pure, like the snow that had fallen and covered Moonbeam Mountain in seemingly innocent drifts.

But this was what she needed to remember about nature.

It could be beautiful and compelling.

And in the blink of an eye it could turn into a devastating, ugly surge of energy that wrecked everything in its path.

Jacey closed her eyes.

"Can you take me straight to the airport?" she said wearily.

"When's your flight?"

She made a great show of looking at her phone. "In a few hours."

This was a complete lie. The truth was worse, though. She had been so lost in love she had not done anything so practical as rebook her flight when their original exit from Moonbeam had been blocked.

She pretended to look at her phone for a while longer. She actually opened a game app on it—had this silliness actually given her pleasure once? Now she could not even concentrate on it, though she pretended to play. And then she gave up on that and opened her emails.

It was probably costing her the earth, using up data like this, and it was ultimately a waste, since she couldn't focus on one single email.

All that pretense added to her sense of being weighed down with weariness. She closed her eyes. And then she slept with the exhaustion of one who has been through a natural disaster. And who has survived.

But just barely.

CHAPTER SIXTEEN

JACEY'S WORDS PLAYED over and over again in Trevor's head.

And what did I get from you? Nothing.

That wasn't precisely true, but he was wise enough to know it was true in all the ways that mattered.

Trevor took the Stony Trail exit and looped around the city, so that he could come at the Calgary International Airport without heavy traffic and the kind of stops and starts that were sure to wake Jacey.

He glanced over at her.

Unlike the first time she had fallen asleep in his vehicle, her head coming to rest against his arm, she was deliberately avoiding contact with him. Her head was up against the passenger-side window, her neck crooked at an uncomfortable-looking angle. But he knew she would prefer that to touching him, and who could blame her?

Her face in sleep was troubled, but no less beautiful for it.

Jacey Tremblay loved him.

And there was not a doubt in his mind that he loved her. She was right; she had given him everything, shown him all of who she was: sweetly strong, loyal, fun loving, adventurous.

Then why was he letting her go?

Not for any of the reasons she thought.

Not because of Caitlyn, or not directly, anyway. Caitlyn would have wanted him to move on. He even wondered if she might have had a plan, two years ago, when she set the wheels in motion for this time for him and Jacey to be together.

But indirectly, it was because of Caitlyn. She had given him an intimate relationship with pain. Here was *his* truth. Time did not heal all wounds.

Time, if anything, sharpened awareness.

And this was his awareness: he had given his beautiful wife every single thing any woman could ever have wanted. He had given her 100 percent of himself and every material desire she had ever had had been fulfilled. He had given with a glad heart and a sense of pride all that his worldly accomplishments allowed him to give to her.

And yet, in the end, he had not been able to give her the child her soul yearned for. He had lived with her daily heartbreak until they had found out the awful truth. The awful truth—the other thing he could not protect her from.

So he was not letting Jacey go because he did

not love her. The exact opposite was true. He was letting her go because he did.

He was letting her go because he knew a secret most men were blissfully unaware of: men were powerless over the caprice of life.

He was damaged—irreparably—by that knowledge. The thought of ever trying for another baby—and didn't Jacey deserve a house full of chubby, laughing babies?—filled him with a nameless terror.

Trevor would prefer Jacey didn't know that about him. That she be left thinking of him as they had been allowed to be for those precious days at Moonbeam. Carefree. Fun loving. Fearless.

She never needed to know what it had cost him to say those words.

I can't.

As soon as he slowed at the airport turnoff, she woke up, just as she had when he slowed at the Banff gates.

With an ache, he remembered her wonder that day.

But now was not the time to remember how going through those gates into Banff National Park had been symbolic of all the doors that had opened in her, revealing her great capacity for life, for bravery, for discovery, for sensuality.

For love.

He steeled himself against the memories that had begun when they had braved driving through that first squall to enter a brand-new world. A world of laughter, of playfulness, of connection. A world that made him so achingly aware of how empty his world had been.

And that was the world he was returning to.

He could change it all. Right now. He wanted to. He wanted to be with her; *don't go.*

But this time the only force of nature he could blame for being weak when he so badly needed to be strong, would be the one raging within him.

Wanting her.

Wanting every single thing about her. Her laughter. Her warmth. Her bravery. But in the end, wasn't every single one of those things about what she could give him?

What could he give her? Brokenness. Cynicism. An awareness that could never go away, not now, of the potential of life—of love—to devastate and destroy.

He forced himself not to look at her again, though even not looking at her, he drank in the sound of her breathing as if it were water, and he would never have it again.

As he approached the airport, he thankfully needed to focus on the road, on the signage, the lights, the traffic.

And not the fact that goodbye was coming.

He took the loop that pointed to short-term parking. Now was the time to remember only one thing: the trust in her eyes. Jacey trusted him to do the right thing.

He hadn't done the right thing. Chasing her around the mountain, around their suite, holding her, loving her...he'd been weak when he wanted to be strong. He had to fix that now. It felt as if Humpty Dumpty had fallen off the wall and he had to try and put the pieces back the way they were before.

"I'll just park here and—"

"No," she snapped. "Just leave me in the drop-off zone."

She was so angry.

No, hurt. And it was coming out as anger.

"If I park, I can help you with your bag," he said, trying for a reasonable, even tone. He looked in the rearview mirror at the suitcase on the backseat, the one that should have warned him, right from the start, Jacey was not as she appeared.

She was as bold and as adventurous as that bag had hinted. But she was also talented and brilliant, deep and sensitive. The past few days at Moonbeam had proven that beyond the shadow of a doubt.

"I don't need your help." And then in a smaller voice, "Please, don't."

And he got it then. He was trying to hold off that moment when he said goodbye to her, and she wanted the exact opposite: *Please don't drag it out. Please don't make it worse.*

Trevor was not sure he had ever despised himself as much as he did in this moment. He'd seen her so completely over the past few days. How could he have not known taking her as a lover would destroy her?

He'd nearly made it. He'd nearly managed to be the better man his wife had always hoped he would be.

Damn avalanche.

He pulled over in the drop-off zone. Despite her protest, he got out. She was trying to wrestle her bag out of the backseat, but it was too big for her, and stuck at an awkward angle in the door.

He reached over her, took it with one hand, yanked and set it in front of her.

She glared at him for the ease with which he'd accomplished that.

"Jacey," he said, "it isn't about you. It's about me."

She looked as if she was considering slapping him. He almost wished she would. He deserved it. It would let the pain they were both feeling out, given it physical weight.

But she didn't slap him. As he'd suspected, her careful control hurt him worse than the slap ever could.

"Thank you," she said, pulling the handle up on her suitcase, her voice icy with sarcasm. "*It isn't about you. It's about me.* The worst and least original brush-off in history."

Trevor wanted to take her and hold her, to taste

her lips one last time, to put his finger under her chin and force her to look in his eyes.

She would see the truth if she looked in his eyes.

It *really* wasn't about her. It was about him *knowing*, as only one who had loved and lost could know, that the goodbye was inevitable between them.

If they felt so strongly after just a few days that the word *love* had whispered off her lips, what would it be like to say goodbye after a year? Five years? A lifetime?

This was his gift of love returned to her, though she must never see it.

That he *knew* the terrible price of love and could not ask her to pay it.

"Goodbye," he said softly. She didn't answer. When he got back in his vehicle, Trevor could not resist one glance back at her.

She was walking away, her chin high, her spine straight, that crazily colored suitcase trailing along behind her.

And though he waited and waited, some part of him hoping for one last glimpse of her so-familiar face, she never looked back.

A word whispered through him.
Beloved.

She would not sulk, Jacey told herself firmly, fitting her key in the door of her apartment the next morning, and shoving the mail that had gathered in with her foot.

She'd had to wait to get on a flight, stand-by. She'd spent a very uncomfortable evening in the Calgary International Airport.

She would not indulge in that ice cream she knew was in the freezer. Nor would she put on her pajamas and while away days watching movies.

She would not be pathetic.

Having vowed that, she stepped over the mound of mail and entered her apartment. It was tiny. After Trevor's house and the suite at Moonbeam Manor, it looked particularly humble. She could see the whole thing from the doorway. Morning light was battling past the apartment next door to create a meager sliver across the sofa.

She looked at that piece of furniture with the affection one might reserve for the boy they had had a crush on in grade two. She realized how silly it was that, once upon a time—a different lifetime ago—she had thought you could make a statement about who you were with a sofa. She picked up her mail and threw it on the kitchen table.

She went through to the sofa and hoisted her suitcase up on it. She glared at that, too.

A luggage choice did not make you bold! Though possibly, it and the sofa, hinted at something…

"Oh, to hell with it," she said. She was tired

and crabby and she did not want to decipher secret messages from past choices. She went and got the ice cream from the freezer and didn't bother with a bowl.

Squishing in beside the luggage on her silly statement-piece couch, she opened the container. She dug straight into it with a spoon.

She only ate a few bites before she burst into tears. There was not enough ice cream in the world to fill the hole in her that needed to be filled.

Nor was a sofa or a daring luggage choice going to fill that place inside her.

Tears streaming, she remembered. She remembered four days of feeling filled to the top. Of feeling as whole as she had ever felt in her entire life.

Four days of exquisite joy. Four days of the exhilarating discovery of what it meant to be brave. Four days of living life flat out. Four days of being so awake, the very spark of life surging through her veins as essential blood.

Now what?

She thought of the days stretching ahead of her. They seemed endless and uninteresting. She got up off the couch and wandered into her bedroom.

There were the new pajamas with kittens frolicking.

Pathetic pajamas for a grown woman. Not the pajamas of a woman who had loved so passionately, so intensely, it had felt as if the love could burn down the whole world around her.

Which was exactly what it had done!

She put on the pajamas as resignation set in. She had, for a few days, tried on a different personality. That didn't make it real.

Trevor had probably seen right through her. And known all that boldness would wear off, and underneath it would be a dull music teacher who wore cat pajamas that were a pretty accurate reflection of who and what she really was.

A scaredy-cat.

She pulled back her covers, exhausted, but she couldn't sleep. She realized she felt really, really angry at Caitlyn.

Why had her friend done this to her? To them?

And worse, had she betrayed her friend by sleeping with her husband? Not just sleeping with him. Devouring him. Letting him be the sun that her whole world circled around.

When Caitlyn was writing that letter, she had only wanted them to return to normal, to have fun. Couldn't she see the danger involved in putting them together? Maybe she hadn't. Maybe she had thought Jacey was just not the type Trevor would *ever* go for. The mousy little music teacher.

Jacey frowned, thinking of that.

That might be how Jacey had seen herself, but the fact was, Caitlyn had *never* seen her like that. As best friends do, it had often seemed to Jacey as if Caitlyn held a vision for her that she did not see for herself.

Mighty, Caitlyn used to say to and of her.

And usually in a moment when Jacey wasn't seeing herself as mighty at all! Like the time they'd gone to the climbing wall and Jacey had only ascended a quarter of the wall before she had backed off, gone back down trembling.

She had seen it as failure, but Caitlyn hadn't. "Don't you see it's more of a win for you to go a quarter of the way up, than for me to go to the top and back a dozen times?"

Or like that time they'd been walking on a path and that dog had come out of nowhere, snarling and baring its teeth at them, and Jacey had held Caitlyn when she tried to turn and run, stamped her foot, said in a voice not her own, *Get! Or you'll be dealing with me.*

She had practically had post-traumatic stress over it afterward, but Caitlyn had looked at her with that sweet smile that said, *I see you.*

That was what she missed most about her friend.

That sense that somebody saw her. That sense that someone held tight to who she really was, even when she had lost it.

She remembered, suddenly, something Caitlyn had said to her on her and Trevor's wedding day, before the ceremony.

Caitlyn had been trembling with love and excitement.

And yet, even on that day—a day that could

have been all about the bride—Caitlyn had not been like that. The comfort of her guests had come first. She had chosen dresses that her wedding party *liked.* In lieu of gifts, she had asked people to make donations to a camp for disabled children.

As they had stood in that room, making the final adjustments to her dress, she had taken Jacey by both her hands and looked deep into her eyes.

"I'm the luckiest woman on earth," she had whispered. "Oh, Jacey, I wish you could feel this way, too."

Caitlyn had loved her so much she had wanted Jacey to find what she had found.

Was there a hidden motive in that dying wish that Caitlyn had bestowed on them? Had she hoped that bringing Jacey and Trevor together would lead to something? Had Caitlyn, always so spookily intuitive, even more so in the last days and week of her life, wondered about *possibility*?

Hadn't the past few days felt as if Trevor *had* seen her in the same way Caitlyn had? Not just seen Jacey's potential, but drawn it out of her, made her into the very person Caitlyn had always insisted was there?

No, that was craziness.

Wasn't it?

Or was that what love did?

Over the next few days Jacey canceled her

classes and her students. She sat around in her pajamas and ate ice cream. She watched movies.

Caitlyn's letter had only postponed the misery, and now it felt as if Jacey was grieving two losses.

But even as she went through the motions of despair, Jacey slowly arrived at the awareness she was not the same person she had been before she had gone to Banff with Trevor.

She was changed from the person she had been when she left this apartment just a few short days ago.

She was completely and irrevocably changed.

It might be a tired metaphor, and yet she felt like the caterpillar who had broken out of the cocoon; she felt as if that struggle had made her stronger and better than she had ever been before.

Once upon a time, when she was a different person, she had naively believed that buying a couch or picking a suitcase could change who you were, could fill some gaping hole within you.

Now, slowly, Jacey came to a new conclusion.

You didn't go to a man like Trevor with holes that needed to be filled. You went to a man like that already filled to the top, and you gave him that gift that overflowed out of you.

She saw her life in a raw, new light.

She saw herself as constantly waiting for the approval that never came. She had been like a storybook damsel in distress waiting for a rescue. Why had she never looked for ways to rescue herself?

She had wanted her father and Bruce to love her.

As if, as a result of their love, she would feel lovable.

But if she first didn't love herself, if she didn't see herself as valuable, how could she possibly expect others to see that?

Trevor's rejection wasn't an excuse to lose herself in ice cream and movies! It was a reason to grow! To become…to become the person Moonbeam Mountain had hinted she could be. To become the person she had always seen reflected back at her in Caitlyn's steady gaze.

A little voice in the back of her mind whispered, *someone who is worthy.*

It didn't even sound like her own voice. It sounded like Caitlyn's.

Worthy of love.

And it seemed to defeat the purpose of her discovery to even ask where Trevor fit into that equation, or if he did at all.

Maybe Trevor was lost to her, but she did not want to lose the lessons she had learned on that mountain; lessons it felt as if her friend Caitlyn, defying death, had given her.

And given Trevor, too, even if he chose to reject it. But Jacey did not want to lose—ever—

the gift that loving him, even so very briefly, had given her.

She didn't ever want to lose the intensity with which she had lived those few days. She didn't want to live in a state of being constantly vigilant, watching for and waiting for the next inevitable catastrophe.

Living like that hadn't kept her safe! It had made her a prisoner.

She had been held prisoner by the insecurities that felt as if they had dogged her all the days of her life, since she had sat in front of that audience, as a twelve-year-old, and not met a single expectation, not even her own.

Failure.

The reoccurring theme of her life.

Had she inadvertently passed that on to her most promising student? It seemed like as good a place as any to begin addressing her issues.

She called Johnny. His phone rang for a very long time. She reached the conclusion he was not going to speak to her—the one responsible for his shattered dream—and rehearsed a compelling message that would make him call her back. Then, he answered, breathless.

"Miss T! Hi! I almost didn't answer and then I saw it was you."

He sounded *happy* to hear from her; it sounded as if he'd answered because it was her. The engineer of his defeat, she told herself, before she made too much of his enthusiastic greeting.

"I've been thinking of you," Jacey told him. "How are you?"

"I'm doing great!" he said.

This was so far from the brooding-in-the-basement-nursing-his-wounds picture she had formed, that she actually laughed.

"It's nice to hear you laugh," he said. "I wondered what it sounded like."

"I never laughed in the two years we worked together?"

"Well, not like that. Sometimes when I hit a sour note you'd kind of bray."

Bray?

"You were always so serious. I mean, I liked you, but it was as if I was getting ready to play at a funeral. Which the CABA audition sort of was."

He was right about the audition for the Canadian Academy for the Betterment of the Arts. It had been the death of his career. Though she was shocked that she'd come across as so humorless.

"That's what I phoned about. I've been thinking about the audition," she said.

"Oh, I try not to think about that. At all."

Of course he wouldn't. He was young! Who sat around contemplating the death of their dreams?

She had.

Since she was twelve years old she had thought about that failure almost every day.

But now that she thought about it, had it really been the death of her dream? Or the death of her father's dreams? The death of his hopes for her?

In the same way her marriage had been the death of her most dearly held fantasy: happily ever after.

"Look, I know where we went wrong," she told Johnny.

She was met with silence, except for a loud banging noise in his background that made her jump. Were people yelling?

"Where we went wrong?" he asked, likely distracted by all that noise.

"Technically, Johnny, you're a superb pianist, but I feel as if I failed to allow you to imbue that Chopin piece with the intensity—the passion— it deserved."

There were those noises again. Banging. Shouting.

"Miss Tremblay, it's not like that."

She rushed on. "I failed you. But I'm sure I can make it right. I'll work with you for free if you want to try again."

"Miss Tremblay," he said, "you've got this all wrong."

CHAPTER SEVENTEEN

"I DON'T UNDERSTAND," Jacey said slowly.

"It wasn't about you," Johnny said.

Hadn't she heard those very words quite recently?

"I blew the audition. I blew it on purpose."

"What?" She thought of all those hours. All that work. Sometimes her back actually hurt at the end of a session, from leaning over the piano for so long, forgetting time. "You can't mean that."

He was just trying to let her, the humorless, laughter-deprived piano teacher, off the hook. He was being noble, the poor kid.

She was changed! And she could change his music. "Let's try again."

"I don't want to try again," Johnny told her, the firmness of his tone very grown-up, and letting Jacey know he wasn't letting her off the hook, because he didn't see her as being responsible for his failure in the first place.

"But—"

"It was never what I wanted."

Now that she thought about it, Johnny Jordan didn't really seem like a kid anymore, either.

"It wasn't?"

"Not even close. It's what everyone else wanted for me. But I just wanted to be a regular guy. I'm playing hockey."

Those were the sounds she could hear in the background: hard pucks hitting side boards, skates scraping on ice, young men shouting.

"My parents wouldn't let me play hockey," he told her, "because of my hands. They were worried about me hurting my hands. But I've wanted to play all my life. I'm late to it. Most of these guys have been playing since they were five. I'm the worst one on the team, but I'm getting better every day. And I love it."

In that quiet statement, Jacey heard the very intensity—the passion—in his voice that she had mistakenly thought she had failed to give him.

"I gotta go. My line is on. Hey! I'm glad you phoned." He hung up without saying goodbye.

She looked thoughtfully at her phone for a long time before sliding it into her pocket.

It was the second time in a very short period that she had been given the same message.

It's not about you. It's about me.

The first time, delivered by Trevor, Jacey had dismissed it as the least original brush-off line ever.

But what if it was true?

And what if it was true, not just about Trevor, but about all the things that she had taken responsibility for—the list of failures she had allowed to shape her?

The list of failures that she had allowed to make her timid instead of bold. That had made her afraid to try new things in case she failed yet again.

There was a world waiting for her to discover it! A world waiting to show her what made her passionate. A world that would put that enthusiasm in her voice, the way she had just heard it in Johnny's.

She wanted to feel the way she had felt at Moonbeam. Intensely alive. On fire with life. It couldn't just be because of the way Trevor made her feel, even though just thinking about the way Trevor made her feel made her tingle.

But in the end, it had to be about the way she felt about herself.

"The world awaits you," she said out loud, and then louder.

She noticed a catalog peeking out from under the mail she had deposited on her kitchen table. She went over to the table and slid it out.

It was a list of winter activities and courses being offered within the community.

Beat the Winter Doldrums.

She flicked open the first page. The activities

were listed alphabetically. Bread making. Calligraphy. Crochet. Doughnut Basics. Doll making.

She flicked ahead a few pages.

Her heart began to pound in her throat.

Skydiving.

Jacey tried to turn the page, but her hand seemed to be frozen.

She read: *You'll never feel as alive as you do when you and your tandem instructor leap into the big blue and let gravity do the rest!*

She was afraid of heights!

It was not a good idea, part of her insisted primly, to get that *never so alive* thrill from tempting death.

Or from taking on lovers.

If she looked at it rationally, trying to get a sense of herself from skydiving wasn't that different than trying to get a sense of herself from buying a sofa.

Except buying a sofa didn't challenge fear.

It made a bold statement, without being bold at all.

Before she could talk herself out of it, before she could come up with a zillion excuses to find a different way to live fully and boldly, she picked up her phone again.

"Go away," Trevor called from his prone position on the couch. It was the Masters at Augustus.

Who would have the unmitigated gall to interrupt this event?

He hunkered down. The new kid looked like he might birdie—

The knock came again, persistent.

He got up, resigned, and went to the door. He threw it open.

And *she* was there. Jacey. The one he thought of, longed for, fought his feelings for every single day. For the second time in his life, he was desolate over loss.

He drank her in, aware it felt like a miracle to see her again, when he had resigned himself to that never happening. Her hair was longer. It looked good. Unreasonably sexy. She had put on a bit of weight, but in a good way. It made her look, what? Satisfied?

It felt like a knife going through him to wonder if someone else was *satisfying* her. What was it about Jacey that brought out the jealous teen boy in him?

Her unreasonable sexiness, he decided, that men spotted long before she had discovered it herself.

Though she did have the look of a woman who had discovered herself now. How dare she look so happy and alive when he was in worse shape than when she'd arrived here the first time?

Not that she could know that. Ever.

"Trevor! You're still in your pajamas."

"It's Saturday."

"I meant the *same* pajamas as last time I saw you in them."

Did it mean something that Jacey had noticed they were the same pajamas as the ones he'd worn two months ago? Of course it meant something! The awareness had been there all along. And it was still there. The danger between them had not died.

If anything, that look of breezy confidence about her was making it worse!

Despite her light tone, her eyes drifted to the nakedness of his chest. There were memories in her gaze, and hunger. She touched her lips with her tongue.

It made him want to grab her, drag her in the house and kiss her until they were both breathless, until the entire world became just the two of them, nothing existing outside the boundaries of what they could make each other feel.

She had done this once before, he reminded himself sternly, made reality evaporate, made him weak when he wanted to be strong.

"What are you doing here?" he growled.

"I've come to rescue you," she said.

Rescue? *Him?*

"Annoying," he said. "The Augustus is on."

But his heart, the heart that had felt like a stone within his chest, came back to life with a hard thump.

"What is that? A movie?"

"The Masters?"

Some heat sparked in her eyes, turning the green to emerald. "Is that kinky?"

Trevor felt the shock of her asking *that*. The shock and unwanted heat.

"Golf," he managed to sputter.

"Oh, golf." She wrinkled her nose. She looked really cute when she did that, not at all like someone who would inquire about his kinkiness without blushing.

He thought he might be blushing. If he was wearing a shirt, he had a feeling he'd be tugging the collar away from his throat, giving himself some breathing room.

She was looking at him way too closely. As if she saw everything. The emptiness. The months of pain. The regret. The questions. The doubts. The four thousand times he had nearly reached for the phone.

Please. Save me.

Trevor said, hastily rebutting the thought as if he'd said it out loud, "I don't need rescuing."

She peered in behind him at his house. "It looks like you might."

"It's socks on the floor, not a fire-breathing dragon." But the heat rising as he looked at her, as he remembered her, made it feel as if there *was* a fire-breathing dragon inside him.

"Quite a few socks."

"Look, it's a long way to come to talk about socks." On the television behind him, he heard the crowd roar. "You made me miss the putt."

"Boo-hoo," she said.

There was something so different about her. That was part of what was stoking the fire within him.

It wasn't just the new hairstyle. It was the way she was carrying herself. The light in her eyes. That little smile tickling across the lushness of her lips.

He realized what it was. Confidence.

Even the way she was dressed seemed different than what he remembered. Except for her wedding day, Jacey Tremblay had always seemed subdued, the woman who least wanted to draw attention to herself.

But now spring sunshine spilled around her, and she'd worn a dress in celebration of the season, apparently. He squinted at it while trying not to appear too interested.

It was the same color as the banks of daffodils the community association had planted. It hugged the parts of her that had filled out and showed quite a bit of the length of her legs. He knew how strong those legs were, and not just from watching her snowboard, either.

Something clawed at the inside of him. It was more than hunger. Hunger didn't feel as if it could consume you, did it?

Maybe if you hadn't had anything to eat for two months, it did.

But no, it wasn't hunger. It was fire.

"What's with the suitcase?" he asked her, trying for an unfriendly tone, one that would chase her away. For good.

Even as part of him sighed its welcome.

It wasn't just a suitcase. It was *that* suitcase, the one that should have warned him there was a wild side to her that she kept carefully hidden from the unsuspecting.

Now, he noticed, leaning against the suitcase was a snowboard. The design and colors on that were *way* crazier than the design and patterns on the suitcase.

No, no and no.

He frowned at her. He pointed at the snowboard. "What's that for?"

"Uh, isn't it obvious? I bought my own. I found out that the rental ones aren't all that good."

"You've been snowboarding?" He nearly added *since* but managed to bite his tongue. No need bringing either of their attention back to *that*. The logical question wasn't whether or not she'd been snowboarding; it was why she had arrived here, on his doorstep, with her snowboard. And her suitcase.

That was the logical question. Engineers relied on logical questions.

Logical questions kept the world from going

crazy, kept it running according to irrefutable and predictable rules.

"I've been snowboarding lots," she said. "There's a hill outside Toronto. I mean, compared to Moonbeam, it's pathetic, of course. But still, it was okay to practice stuff."

"Huh." She'd gone snowboarding without him. He had no right to feel faintly miffed, as if somehow he had thought that would be *their* thing.

They were not *they*.

He hoped she hadn't been practicing anything else since he wasn't there to protect her from the Ozzies of the world.

"Why are you here?" he asked gruffly, asking the logical question. He drew in a deep breath. "Please don't tell me you got another letter from Caitlyn."

Jacey actually cocked her head at him. For God's sake, it looked as if she felt sorry for him.

"No, no letters from Caitlyn," she said. "Unlike you, I got the message the first time."

Unlike him? He glared at her. "Oh, yeah, and what was that?"

"It was that time can be short. Shorter than we think," she said softly. "The message was to live every minute."

He supposed that explained her snowboarding without him.

"The message," she continued softly, "was to accept every single gift life offers."

He warned himself not to say it to her. But the words came out, anyway.

"I got a message, too," he said. "It's different than yours. You know how we've talked about things that have the potential to be dangerous?"

"Airplanes, bathrooms," she said.

"You know what's the most dangerous thing of all?" he asked her.

"Love?" she guessed, softly. She had no right to be looking at him like that. As if she *saw* him. Completely.

"Hope," he whispered, his voice hoarse. "We hoped for a baby. And instead we got a diagnosis. And then we hoped for a cure."

Tears were slipping down Jacey's cheeks. See? This is exactly what he hadn't wanted. To drag her into his world of disillusionment.

He wanted to stop speaking. But he didn't.

He said, "Right until her very last breath, I hoped. I hoped for a miracle."

The tears kept coming. Strangely, it did not feel as if her tears were hurting her. It felt as though they were healing him.

Then she spoke. "Maybe this is our miracle. Love rising out of the ashes of all that despair. I know it's not the one we asked for. Or hoped for. But maybe this is the miracle we needed. The miracle of believing love can win."

Trevor was thunderstruck. He could feel everything in him that wanted to be strong, that

wanted to stubbornly hold on, that wanted to protect her, beginning to tremble, a structure warning of collapse.

"Look what I have," she said.

He was not sure he would have been surprised
if she pulled a toy poodle from that oversize bag.
She held something in front of him, right under
his nose.

Lift tickets. Moonbeam.

"Plus a couple days at the hotel."

He could actually feel a little bead of sweat
breaking out over his upper lip as his heart, fool-
ish thing it was, leaned toward what Jacey was
holding out.

Not lift tickets.

No.

The most dangerous thing of all.

Hope.

CHAPTER EIGHTEEN

HOPE THAT JACEY was holding, not tickets, but a key. To the way out of his life, layered now, discontent on top of his grief.

He'd felt flat, out of sorts since he'd dropped Jacey at the airport. His life had seemed like a yawning cavern of emptiness.

He'd asked himself a thousand times, maybe more, if it had been the right thing to do, to let her go.

He'd beaten himself up at least that many times for the affair.

Though he wasn't sure if it was an affair, and he sometimes got lost in debates over the semantics of it.

Intimacy.

Event.

Fling.

Hookup.

What he'd discovered was beating himself up, and inner debates kept it all at an intellectual level. It kept it in his head, where he could cope with it. It kept the physical longing for her at bay. Slightly.

The facts: he'd had a hookup, fling, intimate event, affair, with one of the best people he had ever met.

He was in a prison of absolute loneliness and self-loathing.

Jacey didn't have the good sense to be holding it against him, apparently. In fact, she was waving a reprieve in front of him.

Hope.

Trevor leaned his shoulder against the door, just to make it clear he was not inviting Jacey in. He thought it was probably a pretty good impression of a man who could have a casual fling and walk away after.

Without her ever knowing it was for her own protection. Without her knowing about the fire-breathing dragon that was taking in her lips and her curves and burning him up.

"A plane ticket," he said as she held up items for him to see, one by one, "a snowboard, extra luggage fees for the snowboard, a couple of days at Moonbeam. Did you win a lottery or something?"

"In the weirdest way, I did. Remember when I played Caitlyn's song?"

A moment in his life he would never ever forget, but it felt as if an admission would tell her the awful truth. That he'd been unable to forget her, or one single thing about that time they had on the mountain. He lifted a shoulder instead of answering.

"I guess people were videoing it on their phones."

"They were," he confirmed. "I remember that. Everyone was taking out their phones." Except him. He had been so lost in that moment, it had never occurred to him that he could have recorded it.

Could have tortured himself with it all these months.

"I'm not sure I could say it went viral, but it's certainly all over social media."

He contemplated that. He could have been watching her, the way she had looked that night they had learned of the avalanche? That night he had seen her so fully and completely herself? That night that he had seen her soul? It would have been torture, but torture of the loveliest kind.

"Anyway, long story short, a woman saw it who is kind of a big deal executive in the music world. I've got this contract to record it. And some of my other compositions. They gave me an advance. It's a ridiculous sum of money."

He tried to say something sarcastic. *Don't spend it all in one place.* But he couldn't. That earthquake-about-to-happen sensation increased as he felt a brick in the wall that made up his defenses loosen.

"Not that I'm rich or anything," she said, "but I knew right away what I wanted to do with it."

No matter how much he wanted to protect her from the destructive caprice of love, even as his barriers were showing signs of weakening, he needed her to know. That he was happy for her.

"Jacey, that's incredible." He meant it. He could see her flying far and high. He hoped she was ready for it. "I'm glad you didn't give up music."

"I actually talked to that boy who didn't pass the audition I trained him for. Remember my sense of failure? It turned out it wasn't my fault. He failed the audition on purpose. It's not what he wanted."

He looked at the light on her face.

Oh, she was ready for whatever came next. The fact she had stopped taking responsibility for the whole world was written all over her. She didn't need him.

"It *has* been incredible. It seems the more I've opened myself up to life, the more good things have happened to me. Anyway, I have money. And I decided I had to use a bit of it to try snow-boarding in the spring."

"I thought you were scared of bears," he reminded her. He heard something morose in his tone.

"Oh, I am. Terrified. But that's why I'm here. Part of why I'm here." She blushed, and her eyes skittered to his chest and then away. "I remembered you said that. About bears in the spring."

"So you're hoping to bump into a bear while snowboarding?"

"Not exactly. But I need to face the possibility."

He wondered if he lived to be a hundred, and if he saw her every single day, if she would ever stop surprising him.

Delighting him, really.

But no, he could not think of that. Of a life that had her in it, every single day.

"Here's the thing," Jacey said, solemnly. "I try to do something I'm scared of. Every. Single. Day."

He was terrified himself at the moment. Of her. Of this new Jacey.

Only it wasn't really new. It was just as Caitlyn had said. Jacey was small and had no idea how mighty she was.

Except that now, apparently, she did.

"I went skydiving," she said, beaming at him.

He'd given up a chance at happiness to protect her from all the unpredictable vagaries of life and she'd thrown it away? Gone skydiving?

"I want you to come with me," she said softly.

"Skydiving?"

"Don't be silly."

As if he'd be *afraid* to skydive. Come to think of it, he would be, as would any sensible person.

"I'd like you to come with me. To Moonbeam.

Right now. I have reservations for tonight. For the next three days."

"No." He thought he said it formidably, in a way that brooked no argument.

"That's what scares me today."

So he was an *exercise* in fully unwrapping the new her. *Terrifying*.

"Asking you to come with me is what scares me," Jacey said softly. "Leaving myself wide-open to rejection."

She was deliberately attacking him at his weakest point. He didn't want to hurt her. But if he could just be strong for one more minute. One more second. The time it took to say—

"No."

Jacey didn't look rejected. In the least. She didn't look scared, either. She looked like she knew how hard that single word had been for Trevor to utter.

She stepped into him, not the least bit intimidated. He had plenty of time to back away from her, but he didn't. There was no sense in her thinking he wouldn't stand his ground.

She laid her hand on his naked chest, right above his heart.

Her scent tickled his nostrils and her touch made him remember things he shouldn't remember right now, not when he needed so desperately to be strong.

She looked up at him, those wide green eyes

wise on his own, and he knew he wasn't hiding one single thing from her. Jacey saw him. She knew he was terrified. And she probably knew he was on fire for her, too.

"Thank you," she said softly. "Thank you for trying to protect me."

"From? Not skydiving, apparently," he snapped, still trying, but feeling the mortar crumble and a single brick fall with a *thunk* from the wall of his defenses.

"That's what you do, isn't it, Trevor? Protect? When I think back on it, it's in *everything*. Starting with really tiny things like the mittens."

He didn't say anything.

"When I told you I loved you, it sent you into overdrive, didn't it? To protect me from the most fearsome thing of all. And it's not death by bathroom."

Her gaze was absolutely stripping. She saw to his soul.

"You were trying to protect me from love."

"From hoping for too much," he heard himself say. He felt another brick fall, and then another, until his whole wall lay at his feet and at hers.

He felt naked, transparent before her. He felt as if her fingertips were drawing his freed heart to her.

He yanked himself away from her hand on his chest, but it didn't matter. It was too late.

"You see, Trevor," Jacey said firmly, "Caitlyn's

legacy to us wasn't to instill in us the belief that love hurts. The lesson wasn't to avoid it at all costs. She would hate that message. She loved with every fiber of her being until her very last breath.

"This is her message to those of us who remain—to embrace every single opportunity life gives us. And especially this one. Love," she continued softly. "I think we should give it a chance."

Jacey felt as if she had stopped breathing, as if her heart had stopped beating. Waiting for Trevor's answer.

Waiting.

Waiting.

Waiting.

Her whole lifetime it felt as if she had been waiting to know whether Trevor would say yes or no to giving love a second chance.

With her.

This time she knew it wasn't about her. Not at all. It was about him. So wounded on the battlefield of the heart. It would be the gravest act of bravery for him to say yes to this journey when it had nearly destroyed him once already.

She would not do anything to coerce him. To change his mind if it did not go the way she hoped. This had to come from him.

This single act of courage had to be his.

To say yes instead of no.

He looked away. He ran his hand through the tangle of his dark hair. He shifted from one foot to the other.

And then, his voice low in his throat, like a warrior on one knee, surrendering his weapons after a hard fought battle, he answered.

"I think we should," Trevor said, his eyes meeting hers. "I think we should give love a chance."

Every single thing within Jacey sighed with relief and gratitude. She stepped back into him, twined her arms around his neck, pulled his lips to hers.

Homecoming.

She had missed him so much. She was starving for him. The Jacey she had become over the past few months did not hold back.

Her lips sought his, her hands explored the familiar surfaces of his face, his neck, his chest. She demanded an answer, and answer he did, every bit as hungry as she was.

"I've missed you so much," he said, in between nips and kisses. He was a man who had been dying of thirst and she was a long, cool drink of water.

"I want you," she whispered. "I've never wanted anything as much as I want you."

Trevor broke the contact. He took a step back from her. When she tried to move back into the circle of his arms, he held up his hand.

Stop? Seriously?

"It's not going to be like this."

"Like what? Glorious?"

He smiled, with annoying patience, as if he was explaining a complex math formula to someone who wasn't very smart.

"We aren't going to jump in as lovers and see if a friendship develops."

"I think we've already jumped in! We've been friends for years!"

"Let's jump back out. And no, we haven't been friends for years. We had a mutual friend. A mutual love. It's not the same. We have to get to know each other in a different way, on brand-new ground."

She frowned. "I liked the ground we were on just fine."

"Humor me."

Jacey realized she felt distinctly pouty about the way this was going. "I pictured something a little different for our reunion."

She saw heat flash through his eyes—in fact, she was fairly certain he was burning up—but then resolve strengthened in his features, reminding her what she was dealing with.

A strong man. And a principled one.

"We need to back up a few steps," Trevor said. "We need to know if what we felt on the mountain can translate to real life. We need to go slow."

CHAPTER NINETEEN

"I'VE BEEN GOING slow my whole life! What we had on the mountain was the most real thing I've ever had."

"Was it? Or was it an amazing distraction? Did we put the cart before the horse? Did entering a physical relationship get in the way of our getting to know each other?"

She glared at him.

"Jacey, the next time I make love to you, I want it to be deliberate. I want it to be intentional. I don't want it to be an impulse. Something we fall into by accident."

She felt the shiver of his words go up and down her spine. *The next time.*

Still, she didn't want to just give in to him. She didn't want to be the people-pleaser she had been her entire life.

"I'm trying to learn to be *more* impulsive."

"And look where that got you."

"Here?"

"Jumping out of an airplane at five thousand feet!"

"Ten thousand!"

He laughed.

Oh, the sound of his laughter!

But then he became very, very serious. "I want to honor you, Jacey. I want to romance you. I want to cherish you. I want to treat you with honor and old-fashioned respect."

"It practically sounds as if you want a chaperone appointed. And I thought I've always been the dull one!"

"Does that sound dull to you?"

"Yes!"

"Then," he said, "you've never been romanced by me."

She felt the tingle of that promise go through her whole body, from her toes to her fingertips to the tips of her hair.

"What would being romanced by you involve, exactly?" she asked.

"I think it should have an element of surprise to it."

"Huh. I bet that means you don't even have a plan. You have no idea how to romance me!"

"I do. I have all kinds of ideas. I have so many ideas it's hard to pick just one."

"Hmmm," she said skeptically. "Name a few."

"Okay. We could go to Paris and drink hot chocolate at a café on the banks of the Seine. Or

I could take you to *Phantom of the Opera* in New York, and have you hold my hand so hard it hurts. I could feed you She Crab Soup in Charleston, South Carolina."

"Not bad," she said, pretending thoughtfulness, even though the thought of that—exploring the world with him—made her feel as if the fire she sensed burning in him was leaping to her.

Both of them, on fire with life.

"Not bad?" he sputtered. "How about this? A gondola ride in Venice."

"You forgot the most important one."

"Which is?"

"Well," she said, "you've never been romanced by me, either. And the first rule?"

"Rules," he said. "Perimeters. Boundaries. I like it."

"The first rule is that you don't make all the rules. Because, really, hot chocolate in Paris, and gondola rides and the Phantom in New York doesn't exactly sound like real life, either."

"Huh," Trevor said, pretending he was irritated. "What's your idea of being romanced in real life, then?"

Jacey loved this teasing between them, the back and forth banter. It felt so right and so good to be with him.

"You win me a stuffed bear at the carnival. We go online and look up a complicated recipe and try to make it together. We volunteer to walk dogs at the animal shelter. On a whim, you go by a market and buy me the odd posy of flowers. We build a snowman together."

He cocked his head at her. "See? It's a good thing we're doing this. We're already learning we're miles apart in the romance department."

"Is it hopeless?" she teased him.

"I don't know. Meeting halfway could be all right. Should we go to Moonbeam and think about it?"

"Absolutely."

Ozzie was running the gondola when they arrived late in the afternoon. He was so happy to see them he was extra friendly, even for Ozzie. He kept letting people go ahead of them as he caught them up on what had happened in his life in the two months since they had last seen him.

Apparently, he and Freddy were now a number.

Jacey glanced at Trevor, surprised at his patience—no, his *interest*—in Ozzie's life. He was encouraging him!

Finally, Ozzie gestured them onto a gondola.

Jacey ducked through the door, and then gasped, and tried to back out again. "There's someone—"

But Trevor pushed her gently from behind, and she heard Ozzie's shout of satisfied laughter.

It wasn't, after all, "someone" already in the

gondola car. It was a huge stuffed bear, with a bow on it.

And a tag that said, *To Jacey, love from Trevor.*

She took the bear. It was brown and dressed in a toque and a sweater and just about the softest thing she had ever touched. She could hardly lift it, it was so big, but she settled it on her lap and hugged it tight.

"You said you wanted to see a bear on the mountain," Trevor said. "And you said you wanted a stuffed bear. Two birds—make that bears—with one stone."

She thought of all the trouble he would have had to go to, to make this happen. The secret phone calls, the money. It was possibly one of the most romantic things that had ever happened to her.

She decided not to tell him that, after all the trouble he'd gone through, the best thing about the bear was the tag.

Love from Trevor.

"Hmmm," she said, tapping her chin as if she was evaluating his effort. "You didn't win him for me at the carnival."

"It's harder than you think to find a carnival at this time of year."

"I know you'll do better next time," she said sternly. And then, she couldn't keep it up anymore. She kissed the bear all over, and then she kissed Trevor.

"Hey!" he said. "I thought we were going to—"

"Shush. I told you. You don't make all the rules."

"So unfair. I can't escape."

She took his lips again. She made sure he didn't want to.

"I think there's cameras."

She moved the bear in front of them and kissed him and kissed him and kissed him.

They emerged from the gondola, breathless and lugging the bear.

They were at the same hotel, but Jacey found out he'd changed her arrangements. Now they were in separate rooms. She went to put the bear away and change into her ski gear. They were hoping to get in one or two runs before the day was over.

When she opened the door to her room, the scent of flowers hit her.

She walked in, and her mouth fell open. The room probably had two dozen little posies scattered throughout it.

She sank down on the bed with her bear and thought about how she was feeling. She felt listened to, but it went deeper than that.

Cherished.

Moonbeam proved to be the counterpoint to the physical sizzle between them. The mountain was a mistress and her challenges required full focus and attention.

But she was a magical mistress. That afternoon they were above the clouds just as they had been in the winter, and just like then, the sun was brilliant on the snow.

But the difference now was the warmth in the sun. Jackets could be left behind. There were actually people skiing and boarding in shorts!

Jacey and Trevor slathered on the sunscreen to prevent sunburn as they lifted their faces to the promise of the coming days.

Jacey soon discovered her vision of herself flying down the mountain—impressing Trevor with all her new skill—was to be thwarted.

The snow, fast melting now, was sticky and could be devilishly hard to navigate.

Halfway down the run, she pulled off toward the trees and lay down in the snow, defeated.

"What are you doing?" Trevor asked, coming down behind her. He did one of those stops that sprayed her with snow.

Heavy, wet snow.

"Hey!" she said, wiping the snow from her face. "My legs are tired. I need to rest."

He flopped down beside her, and they stared up at the endless blue sky; let the sun touch their faces.

She noticed how comfortable the silence was between them.

"You know what this snow is perfect for?"

"Not snowboarding?"

"Snowmen!"

She cast him a glance. Despite his assertion they needed to get to know each other, she had a feeling Trevor was working through that list with lightning speed!

He kicked off his skis and leaned them up against a nearby tree. Then he came and sprang the bindings on her snowboard.

He held out his hand and pulled her to her feet. She looked at his lips.

She thought, *to heck with snowmen.*

But he let go of her and scooped up a handful of snow. He formed it into a careful ball. The engineer was coming out in him!

He began to push the ball, and the snow was perfect. Each push more snow clung to it, and it began to leave a wide snow-denuded pathway behind it.

She joined him, their shoulders together, gasping, slipping, laughing.

"It's way too big," she told him, when it felt as if they couldn't push it another inch.

"It's never too big," he insisted.

And it turned out he was right, because soon two teenagers who had been snowboarding had kicked off their boards, too, and were pushing that huge ball of snow.

Then, as they started the second ball, a family joined them.

Jacey recognized that, somehow, she and Trevor

were at the center of it all, their glow drawing people to them like nectar drew bees. Soon, the crowd of people had created an epic snowman. They stood back, admiring their work only briefly, and then they created a snowwoman, now children and a snow house for them all to live in.

It was amazing to her how that community had leaped up around them, orbiting their joie de vivre.

It began like that. A magic between them overflowing into everything as they enjoyed the mountain and all its amenities.

Jacey found she quite enjoyed tormenting him—laying her hand on his shoulder, touching his tush when no one was looking, kissing him and coaxing him to kiss her back.

She was tormenting herself, too, of course. Still, this playful teasing sharpened their awareness of each other to that point where it was hard to tell whether it was pleasure or pain.

She took the greatest chance of all. She said the word to him that had chased him away the first time.

Only this time she added two words to it. *I love you.*

CHAPTER TWENTY

Trevor let those words sink in.

I love you.

Without a doubt, the most powerful and the most meaningful words in the universe. To receive.

And to give.

And so he said them back.

He was stunned by how the words rolled off his tongue with the taste and effervescence of the finest champagne.

He was amazed and gratified at how alive he felt.

And shocked and dismayed by how quickly the time at Moonbeam dissolved. Their journey to the airport this time was completely different than the last time he had dropped her off there.

He went in with her.

They said goodbye as if they might never see each other again. He'd never been publicly demonstrative. He was pretty sure Jacey never had been, either. But her getting on the airplane made him kiss her without the reservation he had inserted—with super human effort—into their time on Moonbeam.

She had named the bear Moonie, and as she went through to the secured area, she was clutching it as if it was a life support.

He was surprised that security didn't try to take it.

But no, they indulged her, sending Moonie through the X-ray machine on its own, the whole world bowing to what was so evident in the way she carried herself, the look in her eyes, the glow around her.

Love.

And he was humbled that he was the recipient of that.

But also the slave of it. He could no more stay away from her than the tides could disobey the command of the moon.

He was on a plane, Toronto-bound, the next day.

When Jacey opened her door she was shocked, but only for a second. Then she flew into his arms.

"What are you doing? What are you doing here?"

"There's two things left on your list," he said.

She took him in, and then laughed. "Trevor! You said you wanted to go slow."

"To hell with that. Where's the nearest animal shelter?"

They walked three dogs in Trinity Bellwoods Park. The dogs were terribly misbehaved, pulling on the leads, getting tangled up with each other, lunging at other dogs and barking incessantly.

The park was quite lovely in the spring with some trees in blossom and the grass turning a vibrant green. Trevor was not sure he had ever been so *aware.* Of the way the air felt on his skin, the way the sunlight looked in her hair, the way the slender column of her throat begged for the touch of his lips, the way she laughed at those misbehaving dogs as if they were adorable.

"No wonder they aren't adopted," he muttered when they returned them.

"I thought Casey had potential."

"Yeah, the potential to eat your sofa in one serving."

"You'd probably be happy if he ate that sofa."

"Why would I be? I *love* your sofa."

And for some reason, she looked at him as if he had drawn down the moon and given it to her as a gift.

"Okay," he said, "let's figure out what we're making for dinner. Do you have something in mind, or do you just want me to search for *complicated recipes*?"

"You can't just put in *complicated recipes* and expect something to pop up."

He took that as a challenge. He put the words

complicated recipes into the search engine on his phone.

"You want gnocchi with burnt butter and walnuts?"

"Sure," she said.

As it turned out, the only part of making gnocchi they were good at was shopping for the ingredients.

"It looks like a flour bomb went off in here," he told her several hours later as they sat side by side on her couch. "Sorry."

"Love means never having to be sorry about flour bombs."

"We went wrong at trying to make the gnocchi from scratch." He deliberately mispronounced it, just to make her laugh.

"It was supposed to be complicated. Besides, I think we've got burning butter down to an art."

"Agreed. And we know your smoke detector works."

"And that you're a man who can be counted on to flap a towel wildly at it to make it stop."

They chuckled, but Trevor suddenly seemed somber.

"I can't do it, Jacey."

She looked stunned. "I remember the last time you said that to me," she said, her voice choked. "I thought this time—"

"Jacey." He touched her face tenderly, looked

down into her eyes. "I don't mean I can't be with you. I mean I can't finish the list."

"What?"

"Paris. New York. Charleston. Vienna. They'll have to wait. Because I can't wait any longer."

"What do you mean?"

"If you don't know somebody completely after you've burnt butter together, you're never going to know them."

"Agreed," she said softly.

"I realized I'm being ridiculous with my lists and rules. It's the engineer in me, trying to come up with the perfect formula. But the truth is, I've always known you, Jacey. I knew you as Caitlyn's friend, and I loved you for who you were to her. And then I knew you as the friend, above all the others, who was there when I needed you, when I needed a true friend, more than I ever had at any point in my whole life.

"I know you, Jacey."

"Yes, you do," she whispered.

"I know your heart. I know it's so strong, and so good and so brave. Maybe what I needed more time for, really, was to know myself."

"And do you?"

"I know I can't live without you. That I don't want to. That you have brought the color back into a life that had gone black-and-white."

"Just promise me one thing."

"What promise do you want me to make?" he

asked her softly, a man who would give her the world if that was what she asked.

"Don't ever make gnocchi again."

She deliberately mispronounced it.

He took his thumb and wiped the flour from her nose. And then her cheek. And then he put his thumb on her lip and felt the full plump sensuality of it.

She nibbled.

This was going to be his life. He did not know what he had ever done to deserve to be loved so richly, not once, but twice.

He planned to be a man who deserved the grace that had been bestowed on him. He drew Jacey into his arms and picked her up, carried her through to the bedroom.

"I promise," he said. "Next time we cook something complicated together we're doing pork, fennel and sage ragu with polenta."

He deliberately mispronounced *polenta*.

And her laughter was more essential to him than the air he breathed.

"Let's do something complicated together right now," she whispered, and stole the laughter from his lips with her kiss.

EPILOGUE

Three Years Later

TREVOR STOOD AT the very top of Moonbeam Mountain. An eagle danced with the same fresh, pure breeze that lifted his hair.

The mountain was so totally different in the summertime. Like life itself, it had its seasons. And this was its season of joy and abundance, the huckleberries, like gorgeous purple jewels, were thick on the stunted mountain shrubs. The lush grass of the meadow was sewn through with a breathtaking array of arctic lupines, alpine daisies, mountain heather, glacier lilies.

The Big Dipper Chairlift had been opened just for this.

For a wedding on top of the mountain.

For the past hour it had been bringing their guests up, many of them their Moonbeam family. Since Trevor had purchased a condo on the mountain, he and Jacey had become super close to several other couples including Bjorn and Jasper and Ozzie and Freddy, who were expecting a baby.

A baby.

The thought of a baby, of other people having babies, no longer filled him with sadness, with a terror of hoping for too much. Instead, when he thought of that possibility, he felt a wonderful anticipation of the future, and the surprises life had in store for him and Jacey.

The guests were assembled now, in chairs that had been brought up on the lift yesterday. Not like the grand piano—they'd had to use a helicopter to bring that in.

It had cost the earth to get it up here, but Trevor couldn't think of a better use for money. Why have it if you didn't use it for moments like this? If you didn't use it to bring joy? To share your joy with others? His intention was to make this gathering, this celebration of love, as memorable, as perfect, as joyous as possible.

He could feel his heart beginning to thud harder as he waited, watching as empty chair after empty chair reached the top of the lift, paused, and then completed the circle and went back down, swaying gently.

Finally, he could see a chair coming that had people on it.

She was coming.

His light. His love. His strength. His spirit. His soul.

As the chair trundled up the mountain, he could see her. Jacey, who had once been so terrified of heights, was leaning over the safety bar and looking at the meadows, her own bouquet of wildflowers dangling casually from one hand. Underneath the yards of silk, her legs swung like an exuberant child on a swing.

His mother sat on one side of her.

And Caitlyn's on the other.

They wore lovely spring dresses. His mother had had her hair "done" and was trying to pat it back into place as the mountain breezes messed with it.

Both looked a little nervous, Caitlyn's mother gripping the safety bar tightly. Trevor had offered to have them brought up in the helicopter, but both mothers had refused.

She didn't have a father or a mother, but she had inherited two families, his and Caitlyn's and those mothers, Mary and Jane, had insisted they be with Jacey the whole way, standing with her, and not just symbolically.

As he watched, Jacey said something that made both the moms laugh. She kissed one cheek and then the other, too, taking Mary's hand with the hand that did not have the bouquet in it.

This was his Jacey. It was her day. She could have been entirely focused on herself, and her nerves, but no. She was bringing comfort to the nervous moms.

His father, and Caitlyn's, stood beside him, the very best of men.

"Wow," his dad said, and when Trevor glanced at him, he saw he was not looking at Jacey at all, but his wife of over forty years.

Family.

In the absence of Jacey's father, Trevor had gone to Caitlyn's family and asked their permission to marry her.

He had worried that Caitlyn's parents might think he was moving on too soon. Or that they might believe that he was replacing their daughter with someone else.

He should have known better.

The well of love that had created Caitlyn ran deep and pure.

Caitlyn's parents told him that his love of Jacey—and hers for him—did not replace the love he'd had for Caitlyn, but honored it.

Honored that magnificent entity called love that would not be slayed, ever, not even by death.

Well-meaning people had told him throughout his journey of grief that time healed all wounds.

This was not his truth.

His truth was that love was the balm for wounds. It didn't heal wounds so much as weave them into the tapestry of a life, making it stronger, more intricate, more real, more beautiful.

Love stood as a testament.

It was the one thing that could defeat all the

sorrow, all the pain, all the sadness. Love triumphed, like those meadows full of wildflowers that had lain silent under the snow all through the cold, dark winter. Waiting for spring, faithful in their inherent knowledge, the sacred knowing that lived inside every seed.

The chair paused and Jacey and the mothers got off. If ever there was a bride who didn't look the least bit nervous, it was her. She laughed as the wind caught her hair. It was now long again, and she wore a ring of wildflowers as a crown.

The dress was stunning. Trevor had not been allowed to see it, and now he could feel his eyes smarting at the beauty. In sharp contrast to the mountain's masculine ruggedness, it was a celebration of feminine softness. Jacey was no longer so painfully thin. As she'd come into herself, she had filled out, becoming the woman she was always meant to be before his very eyes.

Her shoulders were bare, her hair touching them, and the beaded bodice hugged her fullness, showed off her beautiful curves. At her waist the fabric pinched in and then flared out dramatically.

The wind caught those folds of silk and the dress billowed out in a cloud of white around her. Laughing, she tried to capture the wayward dress, reminding him of that very famous photo of a movie star standing over a grate.

He knew Jacey had debated the dress, not at

all sure if she should go so traditional. After all, she'd told him solemnly, she had been married before.

But Trevor had suggested she—the woman who had leaped from airplanes and soared down the slopes of Moonbeam—make her own rules.

He saw that she had. And that this time she was accepting—embracing—every single thing she deserved.

As he watched her playfully trying to pin the dress down, he considered the age-old vows he was about to take with her. For better, for worse, for richer, for poorer, in sickness and in health.

He thought, perhaps, most people who took those vows misinterpreted them as some kind of endurance test, a promise to grit your teeth and stick with it, no matter what.

But Trevor saw the vows on a deeper level. He saw that love was not diminished by the many challenges that would be thrown at it. Indeed, it was made stronger as people found themselves, and found who they really were, discovered what they were made of. A smooth life, a life without bumps and obstacles, a life without mountains to climb, rarely showed people that. But a strong relationship that survived storms did.

The wind died then, as if on cue, and Jacey's dress settled around her.

Johnny Jordan began to play. It was Trevor's

gift to Jacey, his surprise for her. The mountaintop grand piano, Johnny here to play. Caitlyn's song spilled out over the gathering, over the meadows, over the mountaintops.

Though it had become one of the most played and well-known compositions in the world, right now, in this moment, it felt deeply personal, as if it was only for them, as if it had been created to bring Caitlyn—whose love had made all this happen—into this moment with them.

Even the eagle seemed to celebrate that there were elements of mystery to this that were beyond the comprehension of all living things. He circled the gathering with spread-wide wings, effortlessly gliding on the air currents, throwing his shadow over the bride, like a blessing.

Jacey went very still. She tilted her head to look at the eagle, and then she closed her eyes and listened until the last note sobbed, haunting and beautiful, over the mountains and the valleys.

Only then did she open her eyes, take a breath, smooth the dress one last time and, finally, give her full attention to him. She moved toward him, Mary on one elbow and Jane on the other.

She had tears, but *that* smile was on her face and *that* light was in her eyes.

That smile and that light held every truth he cared to know.

After the cold came the warmth.

After the darkness came the light.
After death came new life.
Love was that seed that waited.

* * * * *

*If you enjoyed this story, check out these
other great reads from Cara Colter*

Bahamas Escape with the Best Man
Snowbound with the Prince
The Wedding Planner's Christmas Wish
His Cinderella Next Door

All available now!